THE WEDDING CHALLENGE

THE WEDDING CHALLENGE

BY

JESSICA HART

MILLS & BOON®

MILLS & BOON and
MILLS & BOON with the Rose Device
are registered trademarks of the publisher.

First published in Great Britain 2002
Large Print edition 2003
Harlequin Mills & Boon Limited,
Eton House, 18-24 Paradise Road,
Richmond, Surrey TW9 1SR

© Jessica Hart 2002

ISBN 0 263 17889 7

Set in Times Roman 16¼ on 17 pt.
16-0303-58356

Printed and bound in Great Britain
by Antony Rowe Ltd, Chippenham, Wiltshire

CHAPTER ONE

'GO AND work in the outback?' Bea stared blankly at her friend. 'Why would we want to do that?'

'*Why*?' Emily echoed, equally uncomprehending. 'How can you even ask that, Bea? *Everybody* wants to work in the outback. It's beautiful!'

'It's not beautiful, it's brown.'

'It's full of hunky men riding around in hats and dusty boots.'

'It's full of flies,' said Bea, unimpressed.

'Don't be like that, Bea.' Emily abandoned her customers and pulled out a chair so that she could sit down opposite her friend. 'This is the chance of a lifetime! I've always wanted to go and work on a cattle station.'

'What on earth for?'

'Because it's different and romantic and wonderful,' enthused Emily, gesticulating wildly. 'Besides,' she went on, clearly grasping at straws by now, 'it's part of my heritage.'

Bea goggled at her. To her certain knowledge, Emily had been born and brought up in

London, about as far from the outback as you could get. 'Since when?'

'My mother's Australian,' said Emily loftily.

'From Melbourne. It's not exactly the red heart of Australia, is it?'

'Well, *her* mother grew up on a cattle station,' Emily conceded with an edge of defiance.

'My grandmother grew up in Leamington Spa, but it doesn't mean I want to go and work there!'

'Leamington Spa isn't chock-a-block with men who know how to throw a lasso and wrestle bulls to the ground single-handed, though, is it? *Real* men, Bea, not like this lot here!'

Emily glanced disparagingly around the bar where she was a waitress. She was wearing a long, white apron, and ignoring customers on nearby tables who were trying to catch her eye.

Bea followed her friend's gaze. It was a Sunday night, and the bar was buzzing, packed with young people enjoying the end of another great Sydney weekend. As far as Bea could see, every single man there seemed to be tall, broad-shouldered and eminently fanciable. That's if you weren't still recovering from being dumped from a very great height and therefore not inclined to fancy any of them.

'What's wrong with them?' she asked.

'They're all city boys,' grumbled Emily. 'We might as well be in London.'

Through the plate glass window, Bea could see the Opera House, its famous roof lit up against the night sky, and the harbour clustered with yachts bobbing at anchor.

Like London? Bea didn't think so.

'You've changed your tune, haven't you?' she said. 'It's only a week or so since all you could talk about was Marcus, and he was as smooth as they come.'

'Too smooth,' said Emily, remembering Marcus with a scowl. 'And I've learnt my lesson! I'm sick of guys like him. I want a man with a bit more grit to him.'

'Well, if it's grit you want, maybe the outback is the right place for you.' Bea grinned as she picked up her drink. *She* wasn't on duty. 'I hear it's very dusty out there!'

'I'm serious, Bea.' Emily leant forward persuasively. 'It's not as if this is just a whim. Even before we left London, I said I wanted to see the outback while we were over here, didn't I?'

'I thought you meant a trip to Alice Springs and a quick whiz round Ayers Rock or Uluru or whatever it's called now, not stuck on a cattle station!'

'I don't want to be a tourist,' said Emily, lower lip sticking out stubbornly. 'I want to experience real life in the outback, and what could be better than spending a few weeks on a cattle station?'

Bea could think of quite a few things. In fact, just about anything.

'Em, we haven't got long before we have to go home,' she said reasonably. 'There's still so much to see, I really don't want to spend the rest of my time stuck out in the middle of nowhere. You go if you want to, and I'll meet up with you later. We did agree that we wouldn't have to stick together all the time.'

'I know, but I won't get the job if you won't come too,' Emily wailed. 'They want two girls, and if you won't come with me, I won't even have a chance.'

'Why can't they give you a job and find someone else?' Bea objected.

'Because the station is a squillion acres and so isolated that they don't want to risk having two girls who might not get on. Apparently it's a very famous property in Australia.' Emily perked up, remembering what she'd been told. 'Someone told me it was the size of Belgium— or was it Wales? Anyway, it's big, and it's got a beautiful old homestead…it's like your perfect outback property. They're used to people not staying very long, though, but this time Nick says that they've decided to take two friends.'

'Who's Nick?'

'Nick Sutherland. He's the owner—*very* attractive,' said Emily with a dreamy sigh. 'All blonde and rugged and square-chinned…just my type! And if you won't come with me, he'll just find another two girls—I know loads of people who'd jump at the chance of working in a place like Calulla Downs,' she added with a resentful glance that bounced off Bea, unnoticed. She was used to Emily.

'Maybe they'll find two girls who would actually be some use in the outback,' she pointed out. 'I can't see that we'd be much good to them, anyway. We don't know the first thing about riding or cows or whatever else it is they do out there!'

'They don't want jillaroos. They've got stockmen to do all that kind of stuff. They need a cook and a governess.'

'A *governess*?' Bea laughed. 'You're kidding! I thought governesses went out with Jane Eyre!'

'Well, I thought it was a bit odd, too,' Emily confessed, 'but I gather it just means a nanny really. The little girl's only five, so it's not like she's going to need intensive coaching. I think it's more a question of looking after her and keeping her amused.'

Bea began to look alarmed. 'We don't know the first thing about children!'

'It can't be that hard.' Emily gave an airy wave of her hand. 'Read her a few stories, make sure she doesn't lose her teddy bear…it'll be a doddle.'

'Well, I don't want anything to do with her,' said Bea firmly. 'Children make me nervous.'

'It's all right, I'll deal with the kid,' Emily soothed her. 'You just have to be the cook. You know I can't cook to save my life, and you're brilliant,' she went on, laying on the flattery with a trowel. 'When I told Nick that you were working for a catering company, he sounded really keen. He said they hardly ever get a qualified cook and—oh, *please* say you'll come, Bea! It's sounds so perfect, and I can't do it without you. It'll be fun!'

'But we're having fun in Sydney,' Bea objected. 'We've got jobs, friends, somewhere to stay…you can't help but have an excellent time here. It won't be like that in the outback. We'd be stuck in a house with a small child. It'll be boiling hot and there'll be nowhere to go and nothing to do. We don't even know how to ride!' She shook her head. 'You'd hate it. *I'd* certainly hate it.'

'Just like you were going to hate Australia?' countered Emily unfairly. 'You said you didn't want to come and that you'd be miserable, and now you're talking about emigrating! I *said* you would love it, and I was right, wasn't I?'

Bea had to concede that. 'Yes,' she said.

'So why won't you believe me when I say you'll love the outback too? You know what your trouble is?' Emily went on, and Bea sighed. She knew that an answer wasn't required, and that Emily was about to tell her anyway.

Sure enough, Emily was leaning forward, all earnest amateur psychologist. 'I blame Phil,' she said. 'He hurt you so badly that now you're afraid to try anything new.'

'That's not true,' Bea tried to protest, but Emily was on a roll and refused to be interrupted.

'You've got no self-confidence any more. As soon as anyone suggests doing something a bit different, you start making excuses. You wouldn't even buy that dress the other day because it was a tiny bit shorter than you usually buy.'

'It made me look fat.'

'You looked fantastic in it, but you couldn't have that, could you? Because if you looked fantastic, some bloke might get interested in you and you'd have to risk getting involved again.'

Bea took a defiant slug of wine. 'Rubbish!'

'And now I'm offering you the chance of excitement and adventure, and all you want to do is stay safely where you are.'

'I've done adventure,' Bea said, glad that Emily had got off the subject of her ex-fiancé. 'I went trekking, didn't I? Adventure means no loos and no showers and no hair-dryers, and you know I have to wash my hair every morning.'

'And that means Calulla Downs will be just perfect for you,' said Emily, seizing the advantage. 'It'll be a lot more luxurious than where we're living now, I can tell you. It's supposed to be a fabulous old homestead—people pay through the nose to go and stay there—so there'll be adventure in just being somewhere so isolated, but with the added bonus of hot water and somewhere to plug in your hair-dryer. What more could you ask for?'

'Shops, bars, clubs, theatres, lights, music…'

'You can have those any time. This might be our only chance to go to a place like Calulla Downs. You can't just throw away opportunities when they come your way. Seize the day, and all that.'

'I don't know…'

'It's not as if it's for ever,' Emily wheedled. 'I'm sure Nick would agree if we said we could just do a month, and then we can spend the rest of the time travelling, the way we'd planned. We could go straight on to the Barrier Reef. What do you say?'

Bea hesitated, aware that she was running out of arguments. This was typical of Emily. She just went on and on and on until it was easier just to give in and do what she wanted.

Sensing that Bea was weakening, Emily pressed home her advantage. 'Please, Bea,' she said again. 'I really, really want to go, and I can't do it without you. I *need* you…and I was there for you when you needed me, wasn't I?'

It was true. She had been. It had been Emily who had come straight round when Phil had told her that he was leaving, and who he was leaving her for. Emily who had dealt with everything while she was too numb to do anything more than lie curled up on the sofa, too wretched even to cry.

Bea sighed. 'Come on, Emily, you can do better emotional blackmail than that,' she said. 'Why not wring out a few tears while you're at it and accuse me of ruining your life if I don't agree?'

'That's my fall back position,' said Emily, grinning.

Bea gave in. 'For a month,' she said, a warning note in her voice. 'But I'm not staying a moment longer!'

Emily gave a whoop of delight. 'You're a star!' she said, jumping up to hug her. 'I knew I could rely on you. I'll go and ring Nick right now—and yes, I promise I'll tell him we can only stay a month. But I bet you anything that by the end of that time, you're going to want to stay for ever!'

'It looks like being a very long month,' grumbled Bea, dragging her suitcase across to where a row of orange plastic chairs were ranged uncompromisingly against the wall in what passed for a terminal at Mackinnon airport. 'I'm bored already, and we've only been here ten minutes.'

Ten minutes was all it had taken for the plane to land, to let off six passengers and pick up two, and to take off again. The other four passengers had departed for town, the man who had pushed out the steps, unloaded their cases and checked the joining passengers onto the plane had disappeared, and Bea and Emily had been left alone to watch the plane climb up into the glaring blue sky until it vanished into the distance.

Bea slumped into one of the chairs and put her feet up on her suitcase. 'I suppose you did tell this Nick Sutherland person when we were arriving?'

'Of course I did,' said Emily. 'I told him when the plane got in, and he said he'd send somebody called Chase to pick us up.'

'Chase? What kind of name is that?'

'I think it must be his surname. Nick said that he was the one who ran the station anyway, so I guess he's some kind of manager.'

Bea sniffed. 'Not a very efficient one if he's forgotten that we're coming.'

'He won't have done that. Reliability is these guys' middle name,' said Emily confidently. 'He just won't be rushing.'

'Evidently!'

Emily ignored her sarcasm. 'The strong, silent types don't bother with clock-watching. That's what makes them so attractive. They've got all the time in the world, so they never hurry or get flustered. Bet you anything this guy rolls up in a checked shirt and a battered hat and says g'day in a slow drawl that'll go with his slow smile and his slow hands—'

Starting to hyperventilate, she broke off and fanned herself with her plane ticket. 'I can't wait! He'll be all brown and rangy, and his eyes will be crinkled at the edges from all that time he spends squinting at the far horizon.' Her eyes narrowed thoughtfully. 'He might be a bit shy, but he'll be famous for his way with horses and don't get me started on the things he can do with a lasso…! He can rope me in any day!'

Bea couldn't help laughing at her friend's famously rich fantasy life. 'Aren't you thinking of cowboys?' she said. 'In which case, you're in the wrong country.'

'Same man, different hat,' Emily declared authoritatively. 'In the States, cowboys wear those hats which curl up at the sides, but an Australian stockman will wear an Akubra.'

'A what?'

'It's like a cowboy hat, but not so curly.'

Bea was pretty sure that Emily didn't have a clue what she was talking about, but she knew from bitter experience that there was no point in arguing with her.

'I'm surprised you haven't got a hat of your own to go with your outfit,' she said instead, eyeing Emily's pristine jeans, blue checked shirt (clearly specially selected to match her eyes) and the red and white spotted neckerchief. 'I didn't realise we had to come in fancy dress. If you'd told me, I'd have brought along a Stetson and a fringed jacket!'

Emily tossed her blonde curls. 'You can mock, but at least I'm appropriately dressed, unlike some people I could mention! I can't believe you're wearing a dress and those stupid shoes!'

'You love these shoes,' Bea pointed out, twirling her ankle so that she could admire them properly. They couldn't really be called shoes. Shoes was much too prosaic a word for fantasy on heels. 'You were furious when they told you they didn't have any in your size.'

'That was in Sydney. I'm prepared to admit that in their right context, they're fab, but they look absolutely ridiculous out here. I don't know why you couldn't wear jeans at least,' Emily grumbled. 'It's going to look as if you don't know the first thing about the outback, and I'll be associated with you.'

'I don't like travelling in jeans. Anyway, this Nick of yours didn't specify a uniform, did he? He's employing me to cook, not to sit around

on fences looking like something out of a cowboy film.'

'Well, don't blame me when this Chase turns
out to be a gorgeous hunk who dismisses you
as a real city girl,' said Emily with the air of
one washing her hands of the matter. 'You'll
be left gnashing your teeth and cursing your
kitten heels while I'm out learning just how
good he is with his hands!'

'I don't care how attractive he is, I wish he'd
just turn up.'

Swinging her legs off her suitcase, Bea got
up to prowl impatiently around the terminal.

It didn't take long. The terminal wasn't much
more than a hut with glass doors looking out
onto the runway. A couple of single-engine
planes were parked to one side near a water
tank, and a windsock hung limply against its
pole. The sky was a relentless blue, and even
cocooned in the air-conditioned comfort of the
terminal, Bea could practically feel the heat
beating down outside.

Beyond the runway, there was nothing, just
an expanse of flat, brown earth covered with
sparse spinifex grass stretching out to where the
horizon shimmered hazily. It seemed to go on
forever. Bea had been appalled flying over hun-
dreds of miles of the same, unchanging scenery

that morning. For a boring landscape, it was hard to beat. She couldn't understand why Emily was so thrilled with it.

A fly buzzed against the glass, but apart from that the silence was crushing. Bea sighed and looked at her watch again.

'Perhaps Nick Whatsisname has changed his mind and employed someone else,' she suggested hopefully.

'It's Nick Sutherland, and I'm sure he wouldn't do anything like that.' Emily leapt to his defence. 'He sounded really pleased when I rang and told him that you'd be coming with me. I wish you'd met him,' she went on. 'He was gorgeous, and nice with it—and we know what a rare combination that is!'

'If he's so nice, why isn't he coming to pick us up himself?'

'He's not here.' Emily sounded distinctly regretful. 'His wife's working overseas, and he's gone to be with her. That's why they need someone to look after the kids on the station.'

'Wife?' Bea shook her head in mock sympathy. 'It must have been a bit of a blow when you heard about her!'

Emily sighed. 'I know...but I suppose he was a bit old for me. And he did say something about a brother,' she added airily.

'Younger brother?'

'I think so.'

'Married?'

'No. I'm pretty sure Nick said he wasn't.'

All was now becoming clear to Bea.

'Name?' she asked.

'I don't know,' said Emily regretfully. 'I couldn't ask too many questions. I didn't want to look *too* obvious, and Nick didn't say very much, just that he would be keeping an eye on things. I got the impression he might have his own property.'

'Shame. Bit of a waste of your country-girl outfit if he's not even going to be there!'

'Oh, well, there's always this Chase person. I know a manager isn't quite the same but I bet he's to die for.'

'He might be married.'

'I shouldn't think so. These guys don't get out much,' said Emily hopefully. 'I've always fancied having a wild affair with a strong, silent farmer type. Anyway, with any luck we'll have the brother and the manager, so we can have one each!'

'Thanks, but I've always thought the appeal of the strong, silent type was overrated. I like a man who can talk about something more than cows. I'm going outside to see if there's any sign of him.'

Retrieving the sunglasses from the top of her head, Bea settled them on her nose and pushed open the door. The heat hit her like a blow, and even behind her glasses she had to screw up her eyes against the glare.

At least there was no chance of missing anyone on a road like this, she thought, squinting first one way and then another along an absolutely straight, absolutely empty, road. She hoped one of Emily's fantasy figures would turn up soon, as the only alternative was clearly going to be to walk into town, and it looked like a very long way.

It was a relief to get back into the air-conditioning, but both girls were soon thoroughly bored and fed up. They took it in turns to go outside and check on the traffic, but in an hour and a half counted only three road trains rumbling past.

Eventually Bea remembered a copy of *Cosmopolitan* in her suitcase, and she had just lost herself in an article about the joys of city living when a dull drone overhead made them both look up.

A tiny plane with wings that seemed to be propped up on long poles dropped lightly onto the runway and taxied towards the terminal, its propeller still blurring. As the girls watched, the plane came to a stop, the propeller faltered and slowed, and a man jumped out and set off towards the terminal at a brisk pace.

'Do you think this is him?'

Emily sounded disappointed, presumably because of the absence of a checked shirt. He wasn't giving a very good impression of being unhurried either. In fact, even from a distance, he looked distinctly impatient.

On the other hand, he was definitely tall and rangy, thought Bea. Nice broad shoulders, too, she couldn't help noticing. As far as build went, he was everything Emily could want.

'Can't be,' she said. 'He's not wearing a hat.'

Emily was obviously struggling to make the best of things. 'He can fly a plane,' she said. 'That's good.'

If the man noticed the two girls studying him through the big plate glass windows, he gave no sign of it. Instead, he stiff-armed the swing door in a manner worthy of the most harried city executive and strode into the terminal.

Bea gave Emily a sympathetic glance. His body might be good—actually, it was even more impressive at close quarters—but the rest of him was a distinct disappointment. He was just a very ordinary-looking man, with an irritated expression.

She judged him to be in his early thirties, but something about him made him seem older than that. Obviously ignorant of the sartorial codes Emily found so romantic, he was wearing jeans and a dull brown shirt. In fact, dull brown seemed to be something of a theme. He had a brown face and dull brown hair, and Bea fully expected to meet dull brown eyes too but, as his gaze swept over them, she was taken aback to discover that they weren't brown at all, but an icy, almost startling, blue, and very unfriendly.

As the cold eyes encountered hers, she felt something like a tiny shock, and an odd feeling shivered down her spine. Putting her chin up, Bea stared back at him. She wasn't about to be intimidated by a cowboy in a brown shirt.

Chase's heart sank as he took in the two girls before him. So much for Nick and the 'suitable' girls he had found. 'They'll be perfect,' he had enthused before getting on the plane and no doubt forgetting all about them.

Chase didn't think they looked perfect at all. There was a very pretty blonde one, dressed for some reason in a cowgirl outfit, and a brunette who looked as if she was off to a party in a skimpy dress and high heels, for God's sake. She had a wide, lush mouth that sat oddly with the snooty expression she was wearing. Chase was hard put to decide which of them looked more ridiculous.

Suitable? Perfect? Thanks, Nick, he sighed inwardly. Personally, he had them down as nothing but trouble.

Which was all he needed right now.

Outwardly, he looked from one to the other, trying to guess which one was Emily Williams. He picked the brunette with her nose stuck in the air. Emily sounded a prissy, old-fashioned name, and she looked the type.

Or maybe not, with that mouth.

'Emily Williams?'

It came out brusquer than he had intended, and the brunette was clearly not impressed.

'This is Emily,' she said, gesturing at the blonde girl, who smiled a little uncertainly. 'I'm Bea Stevenson.'

Her voice was very clear and English, and Chase wondered whether she expected him to bow.

'Bee?' he repeated. What kind of name was that? 'As in buzzing and honey?'

'As in Beatrice,' she said coldly. 'You must be Mr Chase.'

He raised an eyebrow. 'Most people just call me Chase.'

Bea ignored that. She probably didn't like being associated with 'most people', Chase decided.

'Didn't Mr Sutherland tell you that we were coming?'

'I wouldn't be here if he hadn't,' Chase pointed out crisply. 'I've got better things to do than hang around at the airport on the off chance that a couple of cooks are going to turn up.'

'We've all got better things to do,' she snapped, 'but it hasn't stopped *us* from having to hang around all afternoon. The plane got in two hours ago!'

'Sorry about that,' said Chase, not sounding at all sorry. 'We've been putting a mob of cattle through the yards, and I couldn't get away any earlier.'

'Are we supposed to be grateful that you could spare the time to come and get us?'

'*Bea...*'

Bea pushed her hair defiantly behind her ears and met Emily's pleading blue eyes. She knew it was a bit soon to get into a stand-up argument, but something about this man rubbed her up the wrong way.

'You should be grateful I remembered, anyway,' he said, unmoved by her tone. 'I need to get back as soon as possible,' he added briskly, 'so if you're ready, I suggest you get your things and we'll go.'

'In the plane?' Emily revived magically at the prospect.

'It's the quickest way.' Chase glanced at her. 'It's not a problem, is it?'

'Oh, no, I've always wanted to go in a small plane,' she assured him. 'It's all so exciting!'

Chase suppressed a sigh. One who was keen, and one who was obviously going to hate every minute of it. They'd had both types before, and it was a toss up as to which was the hardest to deal with. The keen ones, probably. The girls who hated it usually burst into tears and insisted on going home the very next day. Perhaps Bea Stevenson would be the same.

Although she didn't look like a girl who would cry easily. Too proud for that, Chase guessed, taking in the stubborn set of her chin.

'Where are your things?'

They indicated two huge suitcases in the corner of the room, and he raised one eyebrow. 'Brought your ball gowns and the kitchen sink, have you?' he asked sardonically.

Bea bristled. 'We thought we'd bring a few books and things to keep us occupied,' she said in a cool voice. She wasn't about to tell him about the hair-dryer. 'We didn't want to be bored.'

'You won't have time to be bored at Calulla Downs,' he said, unimpressed by their forethought.

Bea opened her mouth to tell him that she would be the judge of what bored her or not, but Chase was already striding over to the cases. 'Is this yours?' he said to Emily as he took hold of the blue one.

'Yes, it's a bit heavy, I'm afraid...'

Emily trailed off as he picked it up in one hand and glanced from the red suitcase to Bea. 'Want me to take this one for you?' he asked.

Bea lifted her chin proudly. 'I can manage, thank you.'

'OK.'

To her fury, he took her at her word and headed for the doors, carrying Emily's suitcase as if it was empty. He didn't even have to put it down to open the door. Bea was left to struggle after him across the tarmac. Her case had wheels, but it was so heavy that it kept toppling sideways and snagging at her ankles, which did nothing to improve her temper.

'So much for slow smiles and slow drawls!' she said bitterly to Emily who was doing her best to help keep the case upright. 'This guy makes that lot you see jumping up and down at the Stock Exchange whenever there's a financial crisis look laid-back!'

'Perhaps he's just having a bad day,' said Emily.

'He's not the only one!' grumbled Bea, stopping to wipe her forehead with the back of her arm. The heat was pouring down and then bouncing back off the tarmac until she thought she was about to expire, but she made herself carry on. Frankly, she would rather collapse into a sweaty puddle than ask the sneering Mr Chase for help!

Reaching the plane, Chase threw the case into the hold and turned to watch the two English girls trailing across the tarmac. The brunette, Bea she called herself, was clearly struggling, but just as clearly would rather die than ask him to help.

Well, if that's the way she wanted to be, let her. It was no skin off his nose, Chase thought, but he couldn't help noticing how tired she looked when she finally hauled her case up to the plane. Her face was a bright, shiny pink and her smooth brown hair was pushed wearily behind her ears.

Chase indicated the hold. 'Do you want to put the case in there, or shall I do it for you?'

Bea shot him a fulminating glance. There was no way she could lift the case six inches off the ground, let alone all the way up there.

'Thank you,' she said stiffly, and perversely hated him for the ease with which he tossed the case into the plane.

As if she hadn't been humiliated enough, she still had to get into the plane, a process which made Bea regret taking such a stand about refusing to dress the part. Of course, they couldn't have anything easy like steps. The wings were set high on the body of the plane, and you had to climb in underneath by setting your foot on the strut and hauling yourself up. In her jeans and boots, Emily managed it without any difficulty and settled herself in the front seat, swivelling round to watch Bea's efforts with a smug grin.

Gritting her teeth, Bea tried to follow her example, but the soles of her shoes kept slipping off the smooth strut and she couldn't find any purchase to pull herself into the cabin.

She heard Chase sigh behind her, and the next moment found herself set brusquely aside.

He stepped easily up into the cabin and reached down a peremptory hand.

'Here, I'll pull you up,' he said.

Bea would have given almost anything she possessed not to accept his help, but it was a question of taking his hand or being left on the tarmac. She was very conscious of the cool strength of his fingers as they closed around hers and he lifted her effortlessly off the ground.

Already scarlet with the heat and humiliation, she flushed a deeper and even more unbecoming shade of red as she scrambled up and collapsed in an inelegant heap beside him. Somewhere along the line, her dress had got rucked up and Chase was subjected to an eyeful of her thighs in all their lack of glory. If he had been hoping for a glimpse of slender golden legs, he must have been sadly disappointed. Bea's thighs were absolutely not her best feature.

Serve him right, thought Bea, hastily covering them up. She wished she had taken the tarmac option.

Her only comfort was the thought that he probably wished she'd stayed behind, too.

As it was, it looked like they were stuck with each other for the duration.

CHAPTER TWO

APART from a faint lifting of his eyebrow, which was somehow worse than an open sneer, Chase gave no sign that he had even noticed her legs. He dropped her hand pretty quickly, though, pulled the door to, and went forward to fold himself easily into the pilot's seat.

Bea was left to brush herself down and get herself into one of the small passenger seats behind Emily, who grinned knowingly at her. She glared back.

Chase was flicking buttons above his head, ignoring both of them. Bea just hoped that he knew what he was doing. She had never been in a plane this small before, certainly not one with a propeller. It looked pretty flimsy, too. She tapped the side panel dubiously. Oh, for a jumbo jet, four massive engines, and a pilot in a navy-blue uniform with multiple rows of gold braid!

'Seat belt?'

She started as Chase turned abruptly to fix her with that unnervingly cool blue stare.

'Oh,…yes…' She fumbled for her belt, but her fingers were clumsy under his icy gaze and it seemed to take forever to snap it into place.

'Are you secure?' he asked with an edge of impatience.

'I'm a bit neurotic about my weight and I've got a massive complex about my hair, but on the whole, yes, I'd say that I was as well-balanced as the next person.'

'What?' Chase stared at her as if she had suddenly sprouted tentacles and turned into an alien, which was probably how she seemed to him.

Bea rolled her eyes. 'Yes, I've fastened my seat belt.'

With a final hard look, Chase turned back to the controls, and they were soon speeding down the runway, the propeller a blur on the plane's nose. The sound of the engine reverberated deafeningly through the cabin. Bea's stomach dropped alarmingly as they lifted into the air, and she closed her eyes and clutched at her seat. If she survived this trip, she was never, ever, *ever* going to let Emily talk her into doing anything else.

When she felt the plane level off, she opened her eyes cautiously and risked a glance out of the window, and promptly regretted it. The ground looked very far away, a flat, reddish-brown expanse that stretched out interminably in every direction. Bea could see the tiny shadow of the plane travelling along the ground below them, and wished that she were down with it, instead of suspended in mid-air.

In the front seat, Emily was chatting away, apparently unperturbed by the fact that she was sitting a thousand feet up in a flimsy tin can powered by little more than a rubber band. She had obviously recovered from her initial disappointment and was doing her best to flirt with Chase, although she wasn't getting very far, judging by his monosyllabic replies. After the way he had pulled her into the plane, his strength couldn't be denied, and no one could call him chatty, but Bea didn't think he was quite what Emily had in mind on the strong, silent front.

She hoped not, anyway. She had a nasty feeling that Chase was not the kind of man to mess with. He certainly didn't look the type to put up with much nonsense. Still, it was odd that he was so unresponsive. Very few men were immune to Emily's sparkling blue eyes and spectacular lashes, but Chase seemed impervious to her many charms.

Maybe he just didn't like women, Bea thought. It would be a shame with that mouth. Or maybe he was married after all. There was no reason why he shouldn't be. The thought made Bea frown for some reason, and she leant forward casually, as if to get something from her handbag so that she could check out his left hand on the joystick.

No wedding ring. Nice hands, though.

Bea relaxed slightly and sat back, only to realise that the lack of a ring probably didn't mean much. She couldn't imagine outback men going in for jewellery in a big way. If Emily's description was anything to go by, they were all macho in the extreme and would consider wedding rings something only city boys wore.

Not that Chase seemed particularly macho, but there was something spare and uncompromising about him. Definitely a no-frills type, she thought.

So he *might* be married.

Bea's eyes rested on him speculatively. She couldn't see his expression, just the edge of his jaw, his ear and the side of his throat. He had a good, strong neck, she couldn't help noticing. She'd always had a thing about men's necks. It didn't bother Emily, but Bea couldn't bear thin, scrawny ones. She liked her men strong and solid all over.

How did Chase like his women? Bea found herself wondering. It was pretty obvious that he didn't have much time for brunettes with a stylish shoe sense! No, he'd probably go for a robust, no-nonsense type, she decided. Blonde, probably, with short sensible hair that didn't require washing, moussing and blow-drying every day, and a minimal beauty routine.

Oh, well. Each to his own. It wasn't as if she cared.

Although it did seem a waste of a neck like that.

Bea looked away with a tiny sigh.

If only there was anything else to look *at!* Looking down at the ground made her feel ill, and the sky was just a blue glare that made her feel dizzy. Bea tried looking at her hands, but that was just boring, and it was impossible not to let her mind drift towards imagining how Chase would be with his wife. Was he always this chilly and forbidding, or did he relax with a woman he liked enough to marry? He might even smile. Imagine what *that* would be like!

Closing her eyes, Bea was alarmed to find that she could imagine it all too clearly, and the picture of that stern mouth relaxing into a smile left her with such a queer feeling inside that her eyes snapped open again.

Nerves, she told herself.

'Are you OK?'

Chase's brusque voice made her jump, and she jerked her head round to find him regarding her with a frown. His eyes were uncomfortably keen, and in spite of herself Bea flushed, remembering the wayward trend of her thoughts.

'I'm fine,' she said stiffly.

He had turned right round in his seat to look at her. 'You seem a bit nervous,' he commented.

'I'm not in the least nervous,' lied Bea in a brittle voice, adding pointedly, 'I might feel better if you were looking where you were going, though.'

A half-smile quirked the corner of his mouth. 'This old girl can fly herself. It's not as if there's anything to bump into up here, anyway.'

'Maybe not, but there's plenty to bump into down there,' she said, pointing at the ground.

'Relax, Bea.' It was Emily's turn to swivel round in her seat. 'I tell you what, why don't we change places? You'll get a much better view up here.'

'No,' said Bea, a little too quickly. The plane felt unstable enough as it was without them all playing musical chairs. 'I mean, I'm happy where I am.'

'Are you sure? It's a fabulous view!'

Of what? Bea wondered. Brown, brown and more brown? She could see more than enough from her side window.

'I'm sure,' she said, thinking longingly of Sydney. She could be in the kitchen, preparing for the evening ahead. The catering company had been a great place to work, and no two days were the same. One day they might be doing a five-course dinner for eight, and the next canapés for eight hundred. It had been hard work, but Bea loved it. It had been good experience too, and had given her plenty of ideas for when she branched out on her own.

Remembering the atmosphere of controlled chaos and the surge of adrenalin that somehow made everything come together at the last moment, Bea sighed. Afterwards they would all go for a drink in a noisy bar and then she'd get the ferry across the harbour to the house she and Emily had shared with two friends. Sydney seemed part of a different world from this interminable journey.

The noise and the vibration and the smell of fuel was making her feel queasy, and she clamped her lips together as her stomach churned. Excellent, being sick was all she needed to complete the good impression she had made on Chase so far. She could just imagine his expression if she chucked up in his plane.

At least on proper planes they gave you a sick bag. Bea hunted surreptitiously through her handbag, but couldn't find so much as a tissue. And she certainly wasn't using the bag itself! She had bought it in Italy, and it was one of her favourites.

Oh, God, please don't let me be sick, she prayed silently, pressing her lips together as her stomach gave another alarming lurch. Hadn't she been through enough humiliation today?

Clearing her throat, she leant forward. 'Um…how much longer will it take us to get to Calulla Downs, Mr Chase?'

'Only another twenty minutes or so,' he said, glancing over his shoulder. 'And you can call me Chase.'

Where did he think they were? In the army? Bea had no intention of barking his surname at him, but she was damned if she was going to be interested enough to ask for his first name either. 'I'd rather stick to Mr Chase for now,' she said coolly as she sat back in her seat.

Chase glanced at her again, and then shrugged. 'If that's what you want.'

In fact, it was nearly half an hour before the little plane began its descent. Somehow Bea got through it without throwing up, but it was a close run thing. She was so relieved at the prospect of landing that even the flat scrub below them looked inviting. She didn't care how brown and boring it was, as long as it was firm beneath her feet.

The plane had barely touched down before she was out of her seat belt and waiting by the door like a dog sensing the prospect of a walk. Chase gave her an odd look, as he bent to push the door open.

'Hang on a minute,' he said irritably when Bea made to clamber out. 'You'll break your ankle if you try and jump down in those shoes.'

Evidently exasperated, he swung himself down in one fluid motion and turned to hold up his arms. 'Well, come on,' he ordered, as Bea dithered, torn between her longing to be back on terra firma and an acute attack of shyness at the thought of touching him.

In the end, she didn't have much choice. She leant forward and took hold of his shoulders as he grasped her firmly by the waist and lifted her bodily onto the ground. It only took a second, but that was quite long enough for Bea to register the rock-hard body and the warmth of his hands searing through the flimsy material of her dress. It might even have been that rather than the heels which made her stumble slightly as she landed and fall against him.

'Sorry,' she muttered, flustered by his closeness.

Chase wasn't flustered. He simply put her aside like a parcel and held up a hand to help Emily jump down before unloading their suitcases.

'You look a bit funny,' said Emily to Bea. 'Are you all right?'

Before Bea could answer, the sound of an engine made them turn to see a pick-up truck bumping along a track towards them, red dust hanging in a cloud in its wake. It stopped beside the plane and a man got out.

And not just any man. Emily drew a deep breath, her concern for Bea forgotten. Here was her fantasy at last!

He was tall and lean and incredibly handsome, with just the right hint of toughness. Here was a man who could ride the bucking bronco, and wrestle bulls to the ground before breakfast. He didn't actually have a lasso in his hand, but you could just tell that it was looped onto his saddle.

In fact, thought Bea, the only thing that was missing was that trusty horse. By rights he should have ridden up and swung easily to the ground. A pick-up truck didn't have quite the same effect, but she could see that Emily didn't care. In every other way he was perfect. The dusty boots, the checked shirt rolled up to reveal powerful forearms...he even had a hat tilted over his eyes.

'Maybe this is Nick's brother,' Emily whispered hopefully to Bea and sent him a dazzling smile.

He gave a slow smile in return, outback man incarnate. It was like watching Emily's fantasy come alive, so much so that when he actually tipped his hat, Bea almost laughed out loud. Any minute now he would whip off his hat and bend Emily back over his arm for a kiss before tossing her over his saddle and galloping off with her into the sunset. At the very least, he would call her ma'am, surely?

Instead he spoke to Chase. 'I brought the ute out when I heard you coming in. I thought you might want a lift back in case the girls here had some luggage to bring in.'

Oh, yes, even the right Australian drawl. Emily was starry-eyed. 'I think I've just died and gone to heaven,' she sighed to Bea.

'I don't think he's Nick's brother, though.' Less dazzled, Bea was watching the two men together. They were of a similar age, and Chase was shorter and more compact, but in some indefinable way you could tell that he was in charge. 'If you're planning on becoming mistress of a million acres, I'd hang on and check out the brother first.'

'What do I care about acres?' Emily was well gone. 'Did you *see* the way he smiled?'

Bea was more concerned about the way the men were throwing their suitcases into the back of the ute. She hoped her hair-dryer would stand up to all the rough handling.

'This is Baz,' said Chase, belatedly remembering to make the introductions.

'Hi,' said Emily before he could go any further. Her eyes shone as she smiled at Baz. 'I'm Emily.'

'Welcome to Calulla Downs, Emily,' he said in his deep, delicious voice.

Chase eyed them sardonically. Here they went again! He'd lost count of the number of girls he'd seen swoon at Baz's feet. The little blonde was clearly a romantic like all the others. Baz barely had to open his mouth and they were besotted. Chase was surprised that he never seemed to get bored with all that uncritical adoration. For himself, he preferred a bit more of a challenge.

Involuntarily, he glanced at Bea. A smile was tugging at the corners of her lush mouth as she watched her friend gazing dreamily at the stockman, and the snooty expression that had so riled him had been replaced by a gleam of amusement. Chase was taken aback to see how different she looked, and even more disconcerted to discover that he was pleased that she was apparently immune to Baz's legendary charms.

She wasn't as pretty as her friend, but her face had more character with its dark brows, firm nose and stubborn chin. And that mouth. Her straight brown hair was cut in a bob that he guessed was normally immaculately shiny but which right then was looking rather the worse for wear, with her fringe sticking to her forehead and the rest hanging limply around her pale face. She had been nervous in the plane, and probably more than a little sick, but she hadn't been going to admit it, and Chase thought she was probably still feeling a bit queasy.

She turned her head suddenly, as if becoming aware of his gaze, and their eyes met for a tiny moment. There was a funny little jolt in the air, and he found himself remembering the warmth of her body between his hands as he lifted her down from the plane.

'And this is Bea,' Chase said to Baz almost roughly.

'G'day, Bea.'

'Hello.' Her voice sounded comically high and brittle after Baz's deep, slow tones, but something in the way Chase had been watching her had put her on edge. Retrieving her sunglasses from the top of her head, she put them on and hoped they would hide her expression.

'Where's Chloe?' Chase was asking, all briskness, as if he hadn't even noticed that odd frisson in the air as their eyes had met.

Perhaps he hadn't, thought Bea. Perhaps she had imagined it.

Baz was talking about somebody called Julie, while Emily hung on his every word. And there was plenty of time to do that. Bea had never heard anyone speak quite so slowly.

'We may as well pick her up on the way, then.'

As if the hierarchy wasn't already obvious, Chase strode over to the ute and opened the driver's door, while Baz climbed into the open back with the suitcases.

Emily gave Bea a nudge. 'You get in,' she said, obviously hoping that she would be able to get in the back with Baz, but her plan was foiled when Chase leant over the bench seat and opened the door.

'There's room for three,' he said drily.

Which meant, of course, that Bea was stuck in the middle. The gear stick was set into the column of the steering wheel, so there was nothing to stop her sliding across the shiny leather seat against Chase. She kept edging back towards Emily, who used her bottom to shunt her back into the middle.

'Budge over, Bea,' she said. 'You're squashing me.'

Bea clung to the bar across the dashboard and concentrated on not brushing against Chase's arm, but it was hard when the ute was lurching and bumping over the rough ground.

'Who's Julie?' she asked to distract herself from the solid length of his thigh on the seat next to hers.

From the fine hairs at his wrist glinting in the sunlight.

From his hands on the steering wheel and the tingling where his touch seemed imprinted still on her skin.

Bea shivered, and Chase shot her a curious glance. 'Julie's married to one of the stockmen,' was all he said. 'He's known as the married man, which means he gets a house on the property. Julie's got two kids of her own, but she's been keeping an eye on Chloe until you got here.'

He pulled up outside a low house which looked to Bea as if it had been plonked down in the middle of the bush with an arbitrary fence thrown around it to create a yard otherwise indistinguishable from the surrounding scrub. Three children were playing in the shade of the long veranda, but when they saw the ute pull up at the gate, a little girl detached herself and came tumbling down the steps.

'Uncle Chase! Uncle Chase!'

Glad of the excuse to get out of the car, Bea had slid out after Chase, just in time to see him smile at the child who threw herself at him.

It gave Bea a horrible fright. For one terrible moment she thought that her heart had actually stopped beating, but the next instant it had slammed back into action, thudding painfully against her ribs and sucking all the oxygen from her lungs so that it was difficult to breathe properly.

For God's sake, she scolded herself. It was only a smile! You've seen a man smile before, haven't you?

Not like that, an inner voice answered.

She was so taken up with breathing again that it took a minute to realise just what she had heard. *Uncle* Chase?

Bea swallowed. 'Uncle?' she repeated in a hollow voice.

Chase looked at her over the top of the cab. There was no mistaking the glint of mockery in his eyes. 'Uncle Chase,' he confirmed, the little girl hanging off one hand.

Even Emily was diverted from Baz for a moment. '*You're* Nick's brother?' she said, staring.

'I'm Chase Sutherland,' he agreed.

'We thought you were the manager!' Emily put her hand to her mouth and giggled. 'You must have thought Bea was weird when she insisted on calling you Mr Chase!'

Bea gritted her teeth. 'I'm sure *Mr Sutherland* knew perfectly well what we thought,' she said tightly, glaring at Chase. 'Why didn't you tell us Chase was your first name?' she demanded.

'I told you to call me Chase,' he pointed out with what she was sure was a smirk. 'But you seemed pretty set on calling me Mr. I thought maybe things were more formal where you come from.'

He hadn't thought anything of the kind, Bea thought savagely. He had just enjoyed seeing her making a complete idiot of herself.

Chase put one hand on the shoulder of the little girl in her denim dungarees. Her blonde hair was tied up in bunches and she had an angelic face belied by the expression in her sharp green eyes.

'This is Chloe,' said Chase. 'Say hello to Emily and Bea, Chloe. Oh, I'm sorry!' He caught himself up and looked at Bea in mock apology. 'Would you prefer her to call you Miss Bea? I know how keen you are on formality!'

'Bea's fine,' she said grittily and forced herself to smile at the child as Emily was doing. 'Hello, Chloe.'

Chloe eyed her warily. 'Hello,' she said without enthusiasm.

Bea and Emily exchanged a glance. Even inexperienced as they were, they recognised the mutinous set to that little mouth.

'Emily and Bea are going to look after you until Dad comes home,' said Chase.

'Emily is going to look after you,' Bea put in firmly. She knew absolutely nothing about children, and she had no intention of getting roped in to looking after one. 'I'm just the cook.'

Chloe studied her with suspicious green eyes. 'Why do we have to call you Miss Bea?' she demanded.

'That was just your uncle's idea of a joke,' said Bea.

'Why?'

'I've no idea. It wasn't very funny, was it?'

A smile twitched at the corner of Chase's mouth as he went over to speak to Baz. To Emily's dismay, the stockman nodded, tipped his hat again in their direction, and walked off.

'Don't panic,' said Chase drily, correctly interpreting the look on Emily's face. 'You'll see him again this evening. If you get in the ute, I'll be back in a minute,' he added. 'Chloe, you get in too.'

The three of them squeezed into the front seat and, when Chase reappeared, they set off down a fork in the track. Bea could feel the dust gritting her skin already, and her hair felt awful. She couldn't believe why anyone would choose to live out here. There was nothing but scrub, a few spindly trees and the bare earth, cracked and baking in the heat.

And then Chase swung off the main track, and they suddenly found themselves in an oasis of green. It was so unexpected that Bea actually gasped. Tall trees cast fractured shade over a lawn where a sprinkler flickered. There were lemon trees and great clumps of pink oleanders and purple bougainvillea, and set amidst it all the homestead, a solid, stone building with a deep veranda running around all sides and an air of gracious calm.

'Oh, it's beautiful!' Emily cried.

Bea said nothing, but she had to admit to herself that things might not be *quite* as bad as she had feared.

Chase drove round the back to a big, dusty yard and parked the ute under a gum tree. From this view the homestead was less impressive. Nobody was wasting water on the working side of the house, with its collection of sheds, its water tanks and windmill.

Inside, though, the homestead was cool and quiet. The floors were of polished wood and the furniture was a comfortable mixture of the antique and the modern. Someone, thought Bea, had a lot of style.

And a lot of money.

Chase dumped their cases in a room with twin beds and looked at his watch. 'I'll show you the kitchen,' he said to Bea, 'and then leave you to get on with it.'

Leaving Emily to cope with Chloe on her own, he strode back down the corridor, with Bea forced to trot to keep up with him.

'This is the kitchen,' he said, opening a door into a large room equipped, to Bea's relief, with what looked like the latest technology. He pointed through a door on the other side of the room. 'We eat on the veranda through there.'

'What, outside?'

'It's cooler out there.'

'Yes, but what about the flies?'

'It's screened in,' said Chase impatiently, as if she was supposed to know that everyone in the outback ate on their verandas. 'Now, you should find everything you need over there,' he went on, pointing at a wall of steel fridges and freezers. 'There's a larder and a cold store as well. I suggest you keep opening doors until you find what you need. The stockmen will come over for supper at seven o'clock, so you'll need to have a meal ready by then. Any questions?'

'"What am I doing here?" springs to mind!' sighed Bea.

Chase frowned. 'I understood you were a qualified cook.'

'I am. That doesn't make me a mind reader!'

He glanced irritably at his watch, impatient to be gone. 'What do you need to know?'

'How many I'm cooking for, for a start.'

'Oh.' It was a reasonable enough question, Chase allowed grudgingly. 'Nine of us, plus you two. Chloe eats separately in the evening. She should be in bed by seven.'

'I'll tell Emily,' said Bea sweetly. 'Any special dietary requirements?'

She was looking straight at him, and Chase saw her eyes properly for the first time. They were golden, the colour of warm honey, and very clear.

'Meat,' he said gruffly, annoyed with himself for even noticing. 'Nothing fancy.'

'Well, I should be able to cope with that.'

She didn't even bother to disguise her sarcasm, and Chase shot her a look as he took a hat from the hooks by the door.

'You're not much good to me if you can't,' he said, and went out, letting the screen door bang behind him.

*   *   *

He didn't reappear until six o'clock. Bea looked up as the screen door creaked and then went back to slicing carrots vengefully.

The door clattered back into place and Chase hung his hat on a hook. 'Is everything OK?'

The casual note in his voice infuriated Bea.

'Oh, yes, everything's fine!' she said, tight-lipped, her knife flashing dangerously as it demolished the carrots. 'We've been dumped in the middle of nowhere, with no idea of where anything is or how anything works...and you disappear and just leave us to get on with it!'

'I thought you wanted to come and work on a cattle station?'

'*Emily* wanted to come. Personally, I appreciate a more professional set-up!'

Chase eyed her cautiously. She seemed tense, and he knew from past experience that the last thing you wanted was a tense cook at this stage of the evening. If they wanted to eat tonight, he would have to be careful not to provoke her.

'You seem to have managed, anyway,' he said pacifically. 'Something smells good. Did you find everything you needed?'

'Eventually,' said Bea with something of a snap. If she had, it was no thanks to him!

There was a tiny pause.

'Where's Emily?' Chase tried again.

'Giving Chloe a bath.'

'Has she been all right?'

Bea reached for another carrot, her edginess at the sight of Chase easing slightly. 'She seems a bit…wary,' she said.

There had been a definite sense of wills being measured and in Chloe's case at least, some calculation as to how much she could get away with. It hadn't taken her long to realise that the answer was 'a lot' as far as Emily was concerned.

Still, it wasn't her problem, Bea told herself firmly. She had enough to do as it was. Finding your way around a strange kitchen and producing supper for eleven with no warning was problem enough for her!

She had changed, Chase realised. She had replaced those ridiculous shoes with flat sandals and the dress with cotton trousers and a sleeveless top beneath a practical apron. Her hair was pushed behind her ears, and her lashes were lowered as her eyes followed the rapid slicing movements of the knife in her hand.

For some reason Chase felt awkward. 'She's a nice kid when she gets to know you,' he said after a moment. 'She's had to get used to a lot of different people passing through, and she tends to take her time before deciding whether she likes you or not. I don't blame her.'

'Nor do I.' Bea looked up from her knife and he was struck again by how clear her eyes were. 'I do exactly the same.'

Although that wasn't quite true, was it? She had decided she didn't like Chase straight away.

There was another pause. Bea reached for another carrot.

'It must be difficult for Chloe with her mother being away as well as her father. When is she coming back?'

Chase had gone over to the beer fridge, but he stilled with his hand on the door and turned to face her, his brows drawn together. 'Didn't Nick explain the situation?'

'I've never met him,' said Bea. 'I gathered from Emily that his wife was working in the States and that he'd gone to join her.'

Chase's hand fell. 'It's a bit more complicated than that,' he said slowly.

Bea paused in mid-slice, and something in his expression made her lay the knife down. 'What?'

'Georgie's left Nick.'

'Oh, I see,' she said uncomfortably. 'And Chloe?'

'She doesn't know. She's too young to understand.'

Chase pulled a beer out of the fridge and wrenched off the top before belatedly remembering to offer Bea one. She shook her head and he sat down at the table, turning the bottle between his hands. It went against the grain to pass on Nick and Georgie's private business, but she and Emily really needed to know the situation so that they didn't upset Chloe unnecessarily.

'Nick's gone to try and persuade Georgie to come home,' he said.

To his relief, Bea didn't offer sympathy or sit down next to him and encourage him to tell her the whole story. Instead she swept the carrots off the board into a saucepan and picked up an onion.

'Why has...Georgie?...gone to America? Is she really working?'

'Oh, yes, she's working all right. That's part of the problem. Georgie's an actress. She's making a movie somewhere in Texas, and she's got a starring role.'

Bea froze and put down her knife very carefully. 'We're not talking about Georgie Grainger by any chance, are we?'

'You've heard of her?' Chase took a pull of his beer. 'Georgie would be pleased.'

Bea opened her mouth and then closed it again. Georgie Grainger was not yet in Nicole Kidman's league, but comparisons were already being made. She had had a small part in a film that had turned into the unexpected success of the previous year, breaking all box office records, and for a while the media couldn't get enough of her.

Bea remembered seeing her being interviewed on a television chat show, and how envious she had been of her creamy skin and swinging chestnut hair and spectacular green eyes.

'She's gorgeous, isn't she?' she had said to Phil, but he had only grunted and said that he preferred blondes.

That should have been a warning.

CHAPTER THREE

'I DIDN'T realise that she was married,' she said after a moment. Georgie Grainger had seemed so young and so glamorous that it was hard to imagine her as a wife and mother, let alone in a place like Calulla Downs!

'Not many people did. She was told to keep it quiet. Apparently a husband and a baby aren't the right image for an up and coming star.' There was a bitter edge to Chase's voice. 'Once you've made it, a baby is the ultimate accessory, I understand, but when you're still trying to hit the big time...no, much better to hide them away. They kept telling Georgie that she had a great future. They talked about Hollywood and dazzled her with hints of multimillion-dollar deals. You can see why cooking a roast for the stockmen would lose appeal, can't you?'

Only too well, thought Bea, but it didn't seem tactful to say so. She had never wanted to be a movie star, but she could certainly understand the lure of Los Angeles after Calulla Downs. She'd been here less than half a day and already she couldn't wait to head back to the bright lights.

On the other hand, she didn't have a husband and a small child to think about.

She went back to chopping onions. 'Why did Georgie marry your brother if she wanted to be an actress?' she asked. 'She must have known there wouldn't be much scope for her career out here.'

For a moment she thought Chase wasn't going to reply. He was brooding over his beer, frowning down into it as if it held the answer to her question.

'She was very young when she met Nick,' he said eventually. 'She was just out of drama school and the play she was in folded after a couple of weeks. It seemed then that her career wasn't going anywhere, and Nick can be very persuasive. He swept her off her feet.'

When Bea glanced at him under her lashes, his face was stern and set. He obviously disapproved of his brother's romance. It was hard to imagine Chase sweeping a girl off her feet, she thought. Tapping his watch and telling her to make up her mind would be more his style.

Unaware of her thoughts, Chase was still talking about his sister-in-law. 'I think marriage for Georgie was just another role she could play. She saw herself as mistress of a famous cattle station, and was carried away by the romance of it all. She should have known better,' he added drily. 'She grew up on a property down south, but I guess she thought it would be different here. It wasn't, of course. It was just more isolated.'

He looked at Bea, but she was busy chopping onions and it was impossible to tell what she thought.

'Georgie did try,' he went on, almost as if he had to convince her. 'She used to love having parties, and the homestead was always full of her friends, but then we had a bad drought and things were a bit tight for while. Georgie decided that we should get into the tourist business, and spent a fortune we couldn't afford on all this.' He waved a hand at the gleaming array of kitchen equipment.

'She redecorated the homestead, built a new wing with extra bedrooms, and insisted on employing a chef, all with the idea of taking paying guests who wanted to experience life on a station, but without getting their hands dirty or sacrificing home comforts.

'It's been popular, too,' Chase had to acknowledge. 'We've never advertised, but Georgie had so many friends that word of mouth was more than enough. And then a friend of a friend from her acting days turned up. He'd made it big in Hollywood and he decided Georgie was just the fresh face they needed. Before we quite knew what was happening, he'd persuaded her to fly out to LA and audition for a small part and the whole circus took off from there.'

'Didn't Nick want her to go?'

'Have you ever seen a picture of Georgie?' Chase countered.

'Yes.'

'Then you'll know how beautiful she is.'

His voice softened imperceptibly, and Bea sent him a sharp look. He had sounded as if he disapproved of Georgie before, but now she wondered how he really felt about his beautiful sister-in-law.

'Nick was jealous?'

'Of course he was. Any man would have felt the same.'

Including him? Bea wondered.

'He could see that she was getting bored out here, though,' Chase was saying, unaware of her mental interruption. 'He encouraged her to go back to acting at first, but none of us expected that her career would take off the way it has. Suddenly Georgie's a star, and everything's changed. When this new part came up, Nick didn't want her to take it, and he told her she would have to choose between him and the movie.'

'Oh, dear,' said Bea. She could just imagine how *that* had gone down.

'Quite. Georgie's not the kind of person to give in to an ultimatum like that, and of course they had a huge argument which ended up with her demanding a divorce. She wanted to take Chloe with her, but Nick said that she wouldn't be able to look after her properly while she was filming, and I think Georgie knew herself that she'd be better here until everything was sorted out.'

'Is that why Nick's gone to the States? To arrange the divorce?'

'No, he wants Georgie back. He was devastated when she left, but a lot of hard things were said on both sides, and it won't be easy. He didn't even tell Georgie he was coming. I'm not sure he even knows exactly where to find her, but he was determined to track her down and persuade her to give him another chance.

'He asked me if I would keep an eye on Chloe while he was gone, but it's a busy time on the station, so I said I'd do it if he found someone to replace the cook and the governess who'd both left in a huff. They couldn't cope with the rows. I told Nick we'd had enough prima donnas around here and to make sure that he got someone suitable.'

Chase looked at Bea. 'So he gave the job to you and Emily,' he said drily.

Bea bridled. 'Is that what you think we are? Prima donnas?'

'I don't know about that, but you're definitely not what I had in mind when I asked for someone suitable!'

She lifted a chin in what he already thought of as a familiar gesture. 'How do you know?'

Chase finished his beer and set the bottle back down on the table. 'I knew the moment I saw those shoes you were wearing,' he said. 'They didn't look very suitable to me!'

'Why do I let you talk me into these things?' Bea threw back the sheet and climbed into bed. '"*You'll love it,*" you said. "*It'll be an adventure,*" you said.'

'Well, it is,' said Emily, still brushing her hair.

'What's adventurous about getting up at four-thirty tomorrow morning?'

'Think of the romance, Bea! Feeding the men before they saddle up, waving them off to a

hard day's work as they ride into the dawn...
it'll be wonderful.'

'If you think it's so romantic, *you* can get up
and cook breakfast for them!'

'You know I can't cook,' said Emily, 'and
there's no point in both of us getting up, is
there?'

She put down the hairbrush and began slath-
ering moisturiser into her face and neck. She
was always very strict about her beauty regime.
Bea often thought it was the only area in which
Emily had any discipline.

'I'm so glad we came, aren't you?' she was
saying, rather muffled. 'It's even better than I
thought it would be! You can practically feel
the possibilities of romance buzzing in the air!'

Bea stared glumly at the ceiling. 'The only
possibility I can see is the chance of being
heartily bored for the next month.'

'You're not looking in the right place.'

'The stockmen's quarters, I suppose?'

'You've got to admit it looks promising!'

'*It?*'

'OK, he,' Emily conceded with a grin. 'Baz
is to die for, isn't he?'

Bea considered the matter. 'I can see he's
good-looking,' she said slowly, 'but he hasn't
got a lot to say for himself, has he?'

Not that anyone round the table that night had had much to say much for themselves. Emily hadn't given them a chance. Thrilled with everything, and especially with Baz, she had been on sparkling form, flashing her bright blue eyes at the shy young men who had trooped in at seven o'clock and stood around awkwardly, mumbling names. They had all been dazzled.

All except Chase, thought Bea. She had a feeling that it would take a lot to dazzle him.

'Baz doesn't need all that superficial chatter,' Emily was saying as she got into bed. 'He just needs to sit there and I go all squirmy inside.' She heaved a dreamy sigh.

'I thought the governess always had a passionate affair with the master,' said Bea. 'What happened to your plan to be mistress of a million acres?'

'Oh, well, Nick's off the market if he's steamed off to Hollywood to fetch his wife, and that just leaves Chase, and I can't imagine having an affair with him, can you?'

The worst thing was that Bea could. 'Why not?' was all she said.

'He's a bit of a cold fish, isn't he?' said Emily, settling herself in bed. 'I tried to chat to him in the plane, but it was like trying to flirt

with a brick wall. I don't see him having a passionate affair with anyone. He doesn't look like
he knows what passion means!'

'No,' agreed Bea after the tiniest hesitation.
She had thought much the same herself, but
when she remembered his mouth, she wasn't
quite so sure.

'He's too dour for me,' Emily went on.
'You'd never guess he was related to Nick.
With a name like Sutherland he must be a
throwback to some Scottish ancestors. He could
do with lightening up a bit, if you ask me. It
might make him less intimidating.'

'I wouldn't say that he was *intimidating*,'
said Bea, thinking about the way Chase had sat
at the kitchen table and told her about his
brother's marriage. He hadn't been friendly exactly, but he hadn't been quite as dismissive
either.

'That's because you don't intimidate easily,'
said Emily. 'Anyway, I think he likes you.'

Bea sat up and stared across at her friend.
'How do you work that out?'

'I noticed him watching you at dinner.'

So Emily had noticed too. Bea had wondered
if she was imagining it, or if it had just been
chance that whenever she looked up her eyes
had encountered Chase's cool blue ones. His

expression had been impossible to read, but she didn't think it had been one of liking.

'He was probably just wondering how soon he could get rid of us,' she said with an unsuccessful laugh.

'He'd better not have been,' said Emily, reaching out to switch off the bedside light. 'I've just found the man of my dreams. I've got no intention of leaving on Chase Sutherland's say so!'

When the alarm went off at four-thirty the next morning, Bea sat bolt upright. She had been sleeping uneasily, dreading the moment when it would go off, and now she groped for the clock and switched it off quickly.

Rubbing her eyes, she switched on the little lamp by her bed. There had been no need to worry about waking Emily. She was sound asleep, one arm flung above her head. You could have conducted a rousing rendition of the 'Hallelujah Chorus' under spotlights without her so much as stirring.

It was pitch dark outside and the early morning air was unpleasantly chilly. Bea dressed, shivering. Nobody had told her it could be cold in the outback, and she hadn't brought a jumper with her. The best she could do was a T-shirt and chinos. Hugging her arms together, Bea cast a last, longing glance at her warm bed and crept down the darkened corridor to the kitchen.

The overhead lights were very bright when she switched them on and she had to screw up her eyes until she got used to them. It didn't stop her feeling any less of a zombie, though. Her body kept insisting that it had missed out on a good four hours sleep to which it was accustomed, and refused to co-operate as Bea moved blearily around the kitchen, putting on the kettle, laying the table and setting out cereals, and jams for toast.

Chase appeared just before five, and something about the sight of him jerked Bea abruptly awake. His presence seemed to fill the kitchen. Under the harsh overhead light, his features were stronger and more definite than she remembered, but his eyes were as cool and keen as ever.

As they swept over her, Bea was suddenly acutely conscious that her hair was rioting uncontrollably around her head, that she hadn't so much as washed her face and that she was bug-eyed from lack of sleep. She eyed him with resentment. He made it look as if it was perfectly normal to have breakfast in the middle of the night.

Chase was glad to see that she was up and appeared to have breakfast under control, although she looked less than her usual immaculate self. There was a cross, tousled air to her this morning, and he had a sudden, disturbing awareness that she had just got out of bed.

So had every cook that had ever got up to make breakfast for the men, he reminded himself, but he had never been able to picture any of the others waking and stretching and throwing back the covers with such unsettling clarity. The thought made him frown.

'You're shivering,' he noticed abruptly.

'Of course I'm shivering,' snapped Bea, beginning to slice bread for toast. 'It's absolutely freezing in here!'

Chase was relieved to be irritated by her wild exaggeration. It was easier than picturing her getting out of bed.

'If you're cold, put a sweater on.'

'I haven't got a sweater.'

'You must have something. What was in that enormous suitcase you dragged with you yesterday?'

'I was *told* that the outback was hot,' she grumbled. 'Nobody said there was a danger of frostbite when you got out of bed in the morning.'

Chase sighed irritably and went out. He reappeared a couple of minutes later with a faded sweatshirt. 'Put that on,' he said, shoving it into her hands.

Taken aback by the brusque gesture, Bea stood holding it. 'Whose is this?'

'Mine,' he said curtly. 'It'll be too big for you, but at least it might stop you shivering like a whippet!'

He lifted an eyebrow when Bea hesitated. 'What's the matter? Isn't it your colour?' he asked sarcastically to cover his mixed feelings about the thought of her wearing his clothes.

Bea flushed. She had been thinking how intimate it would be to put on something of his, but she couldn't tell him that.

She pulled the sweatshirt over her head. It was clean and warm, and smelt oddly familiar, as if she wore his shirts every day. As Chase had said, it was much too big for her, but she rolled up the sleeves, very conscious of how many times he must have pulled on the same sweatshirt, of where the material he had worn against his skin was now brushing against hers.

Don't be ridiculous, she told herself. It's just a sweatshirt.

But she still felt stupidly shy as she glanced up from rolling the second sleeve. 'Thank you,' she said belatedly. 'I'll let you have it back when I've washed it.'

'You'd better keep it,' said Chase brusquely. 'We can't have you freezing to death every morning.'

They looked at each other, then away, and then, as if their eyes had a will of their own, back again. Bea was very aware of the noise of the kettle coming up to the boil, of the faint hum of the fridges in the background, which only seemed to emphasise the odd silence between them. It was broken, to her intense relief, by the sound of boots clumping up the wooden steps onto the veranda, and she turned away to busy herself putting on the toast as the stockmen came in.

Breakfast was a largely silent affair, with conversation restricted to what needed to be done that day. The men were taciturn at the best of times, Bea guessed, and she was glad of it at this time of the morning. It was bad enough having to fry eggs for a bunch of hungry men and serve it with grilled steak without having to cope with cheeriness as well.

'We'll be back for smoko at ten-thirty,' said Chase as they trooped out.

Who was Smoko? Bea wondered. One of the stockmen? They all seemed to have funny names like that. But surely they had all been there, eating their way stolidly through steak and eggs. Maybe it was a dog?

'Smoko?' she echoed cautiously.

Chase looked at her baffled expression. 'Smoko,' he repeated very slowly and clearly as if talking to an idiot. 'The men come back for a cup of tea and a smoke in the middle of the morning.'

'Oh, a *break!*' Her face cleared.

'Right,' said Chase drily. 'If you could make some biscuits or a cake for ''break'',' he said, putting inverted commas around the word and mimicking her English accent, 'that would be good.'

Bea had been planning to go back to bed and baking was the last thing on her mind, but when she looked at her watch she saw that there was still hours to go before half past ten. With any luck she would be able to catch up on some sleep, have a shower, do her hair and still have time to knock up a quick batch of biscuits.

'Fine,' she said, catching herself on a yawn.

'We'll see you later then.'

Chase took down his hat and stood with it hanging from his hand for a moment as he glanced back at Bea. She was holding an armful of plates, and had succumbed to another huge yawn. Her brown hair was messy, and smothered in his sweatshirt she looked a completely different girl from the one who had stuck her nose in the air at Mackinnon airport.

'Thanks for breakfast,' he said abruptly.

The screen door clattered shut behind him.

Bea was still staring after him, trying to work out what that odd expression on his face had meant, when a suspicious voice behind her made her jump.

'What are you doing?'

It was Chloe, looking deceptively angelic in pink pyjamas covered in teddy bears.

'I'm not doing anything,' said Bea, eyeing her with equal wariness. She carried the plates over to the sink and dumped them down.

'You had a funny smile on your face.'

Even though she knew it was nonsense, Bea felt a flush creeping up her cheeks. That was the trouble with children. They always made you feel such a fool.

'Can I have a drink?' Chloe went on without waiting for a reply.

Bea's heart sank even further. Where was Emily when she needed her? When she looked at the clock on the wall, it wasn't even six o'clock.

'Do you always get up this early?' she asked.

Chloe looked at her as if she didn't know what she was talking about, which she probably didn't. No doubt six o'clock counted as a lie-in around here.

Now what was she going to do? She couldn't go back to bed and leave the little girl on her own. She couldn't even have a shower until Emily woke up, she realised.

In the end, she made Chloe some breakfast, and sat down to drink a cup of coffee with her. It was light by then, and Bea was beginning to feel that she had been up for hours.

'Why are you wearing Uncle Chase's jumper?' Chloe demanded suddenly.

Bea had forgotten the sweatshirt. She looked down at herself a little self-consciously. 'He lent it to me because I was cold.'

Chloe digested this, trailing her spoon in her cereal. 'Are you Uncle Chase's new girlfriend?'

New girlfriend? Hmm, thought Bea.

'No,' she said, putting her mug down, carefully casual. 'What makes you think that?'

'You're the cook.'

'Yes?' Bea suddenly realised that Chloe thought that she had answered the question. 'Is the cook always his girlfriend?' she laughed.

'Sometimes.'

Bea stopped laughing abruptly. 'I see,' she said, inexplicably ruffled.

She picked up her mug again, determined not to show any more interest, and Chloe went back to her breakfast, apparently satisfied.

'So, was the last cook his girlfriend?' Bea heard herself ask.

'Who?'

Bea sucked in her breath. 'Uncle Chase. Was the cook who was here before me his girlfriend?'

Chloe frowned with the effort of memory. 'I think so.'

Somehow this wasn't the answer Bea wanted to hear. 'Well, I'm not,' she said as if Chloe had accused her of something.

'Is Emily?'

'No!' Bea didn't want to explain even to herself why the thought of Emily and Chase together was out of the question. 'No,' she said again, more quietly, 'she's not his girlfriend either. I'm afraid Uncle Chase is going to have to do without a girlfriend for a while.'

She got abruptly to her feet. 'You finish your breakfast. I'm going to clear up.'

Unaccountably cross, she began to clear the table with much clattering of plates and cutlery. She was about to scrape the last pieces of toast savagely into the bin when Chloe stopped her, shocked.

'We can give those to the chooks!'

She insisted on taking Bea down to see the hens in their run as soon as she had finished her cereal. At the sound of the gate being opened the hens came running, tumbling over themselves in their eagerness to find the scraps that the little girl scattered for them.

Bea calmed down as she watched the chooks, and waited for Chloe to collect the eggs. Really, she must be even more tired than she thought. What did it matter to her if Chase was used to the kitchen staff throwing themselves at his feet? If he wanted to be that undiscriminating, that was his problem! As long as he didn't expect her to fall in with tradition, he could do what he liked.

Chloe found five eggs and presented them proudly in the bowl for her to admire. 'We could make something for smoko,' Bea suggested. 'What do you think the men would like?'

'Chase likes rock cakes best.'

'Then let's make those,' she said, thinking that rock cakes would be an easy place for Chloe to start.

Chloe was thrilled at the idea of helping Bea to cook, and she chattered all the way back to the homestead, her wariness vanquished.

By the time Emily appeared, yawning, the rock cakes were in the oven and Bea and Chloe were both liberally dusted with flour. Bea was desperate to have a shower and wash her hair, and she was taking off her apron and leaving instructions about when to take the rock cakes out when Chase came in.

'You're early!' she said without thinking and then was furious with herself. It sounded as if she had been watching the clock, waiting for him to return. 'I mean, it's only quarter to ten. I didn't think you'd be back until half past.'

She was just making matters worse. Chase raised a faint eyebrow, but said only that he had come back to make a couple of phone calls. 'The men will be back at ten-thirty.'

'Chase! Chase!' Chloe was tugging at this hand. 'We made rock cakes! I said they were your favourites, so Bea said we should make those.'

'Oh?' Chase looked at Bea, who was still half in, half out of her apron.

'Aha!' said Emily wickedly. 'Trying to curry favour with the boss, eh, Bea?'

Bea set her teeth and finally managed to wrench the stupid apron over her head. 'I just asked what everyone would like.'

'Chloe's right, I do like rock cakes.' The keen gaze rested on her face and Bea was horribly conscious of her dirty hair. Involuntarily, she lifted her hand to a smudge of flour on her cheek and wiped it off. 'I'll look forward to smoko,' Chase said in his cool way, and disappeared in the direction of the office.

Leaving Emily in charge, Bea had a shower, washed her hair and dried it carefully. When she had finished, it fell straight and shining, swinging below her jaw the way she liked it.

Bea and her hair had a complex relationship. It was so wildly curly that it had to be washed and blow-dried into shape every morning or it looked awful, and Bea had long ago established the intricate connection between her hair and her well-being. Endless people had mocked her for the time she spent forcing her curls into a neat style, but she was used to it now. If her hair was out of control, so was her life, and that was all there was to it. The whole process took hours out of her life every week, but Bea told herself it was worth it.

At least now she felt human again, and would be once more the calm, composed person she knew herself to be the next time that she saw Chase.

Although, as things turned out, she might as well have spared herself the effort, Bea reflected as she carried a big metal pot of tea out onto the kitchen veranda where the men could have their smoko without taking off their dusty boots. Chase took a rock cake that Chloe handed carefully round on a plate, but he hardly seemed to notice Bea as she poured out the tea. He talked about bores and dams and fences and when they would start to muster, and gave her absolutely no opportunity to impress him with her cool control.

Aggrieved in a way she couldn't begin to explain, Bea sat down as far away from him as possible but, although she tried to ignore him, her eyes kept sliding towards him as he sat on the bench, leaning his elbows on his knees, his mug clasped lightly between his hands. He was listening to one of the stockmen, his expression intent. Their conversation was unintelligible to Bea, but it seemed to mean something to Chase, for he nodded every now and then, or put in a quiet word.

His sleeves were rolled up above his wrists and his shirt was open at the neck. Bea could see the strong column of his throat, the firm set of his mouth, and she found herself wondering about the girls who had made smoko for these men before her. How many of them had been carrying on a relationship with Chase? He obviously hadn't ignored *them!*

Chase drained his tea and stood up. It was the signal for all the other men to get up as well, and they headed back out into the heat and dust. Chase went down the wooden steps, too, but he turned at the bottom to look back up at Bea as he settled his hat on his head.

'Good rock cakes,' he said with a smile.

Quite without wanting to, Bea found herself smiling back until she caught Emily's interested eye and stopped abruptly. 'Thanks,' she said in a curt voice, and began collecting up the mugs. By the time she looked up again, Chase had gone.

'I told you he liked you,' said Emily.

Her hands full of mugs, Bea hooked the screen door open with her foot. 'He likes my rock cakes,' she said dismissively. 'And that's all.'

It took more than a smile and a tossed compliment about her baking to win her over, she reminded herself. If Chase thought she was going to be like all the other cooks who had apparently fallen into his arms, he would soon discover that he was mistaken!

By six o'clock, Bea was exhausted. She was used to hard work, but she certainly wasn't used to getting up at four-thirty, or to the heat, or to the constant background noise of Chloe asking unanswerable questions.

Why is your hair straight?

Why is England far away?

Why, why, why, until Bea wanted to scream. It was a huge relief when Emily, having taken a typically relaxed view of her duties all day, finally roused herself to take Chloe off for a bath. Bea contemplated sitting down to savour the blissful silence, but she was afraid that if she did she might never get up again.

'Chloe is desperate for you to read her a story,' Emily announced coming into the kitchen a bit later. 'Is everything under control in here?'

'Yes, but—'

'Oh, good. I'll just nip and have a shower, then. Baz is taking me out in his ute this evening.'

Bea undid her apron with a sigh.

Chloe was sitting up in bed in her pink py-jamas, books strewn around her. 'I'm only read-ing one,' warned Bea, sensing danger.

Of course Chloe chose the longest, and she was unimpressed when Bea sat down on the other bed. 'Don't you *know* how to read a story?' she demanded witheringly. She made Bea sit on her bed, and tucked herself com-fortably in beside her. 'This is how Mum reads me a story,' she confided.

Bea glanced down at the small shining head. Chloe was extraordinarily self-possessed but she must miss her mother. What would it be like, having a mother like Georgie Grainger? she wondered. Georgie would always be warm and beautiful, and she probably smelt of expen-sive perfume and not of roasting meat and on-ions.

She probably read wonderful stories too, Bea thought glumly. An actress like Georgie would be able to do all the voices properly.

Oh, well, she would just have to do. She had never said that she was Mary Poppins.

She was doing all right, too, until Chase came in, and she faltered in mid-sentence.

He had had a shower, and his brown hair was slicked back against his head. He wasn't a particularly big man, but he seemed enormous amongst the little furniture in Chloe's room.

'I'll wait till you finish,' he said, and sat down on the spare bed to listen.

Bea immediately lost the thread of the story and started stumbling over the most basic words. Clearing her throat firmly, she started the page again, but it was hard to concentrate with Chase sitting opposite her like that. He wasn't exactly smiling, but the creases at the edges of his eyes had deepened and one corner of his mouth looked as if it might be about to twitch upwards.

It was very distracting.

She tried skipping a few pages to get to the end, but Chloe was having none of it.

'You missed a page!'

'Did I?' Bea gritted her teeth and let Chloe turn the page back. 'Silly me.'

Chase's eyes rested appreciatively on Bea's face. She looked a little pink, although whether from cooking or frustration with the slow progress of the story he couldn't tell. It was pretty obvious that she wasn't used to children, but Chloe seemed to have taken to her for some reason. Chase would have expected her to have preferred Emily, who was pretty and lively, while Bea was wary and utterly out of place.

Not that she was exactly plain, Chase allowed to himself. She was attractive enough if you liked your women smart and tense. His gaze rested on her face. The straight brown hair was hooked behind her ears, and long lashes shielded the strange golden eyes. She absolutely wasn't his type, he decided. Too uptight and British for him.

In spite of that mouth, which wasn't uptight at all.

At last Bea struggled to the end of the story and closed the book with relief.

'More! More!' cried Chloe, but Chase was firm.

'No, you're going to sleep now.'

For a perilous moment, Chloe's bottom lip stuck out rebelliously, but a glance at her uncle's implacable face made her clamber reluctantly into bed. Chase bent to kiss her goodnight, tickling her until her cross little face dissolved into giggles.

Getting to her feet in relief, Bea was surprised at how much Chloe obviously adored him. He didn't seem like a man who would be good with children. He wasn't exactly the cuddly type.

Even if he did have a nice smile.

Just the thought of Chase's smile gave Bea an odd feeling inside, and when she saw him grin down at Chloe, she turned abruptly for the door.

'I'd better go and check on supper.'

CHAPTER FOUR

'I HAVEN'T kissed you yet!' Chloe protested. 'You haven't kissed me goodnight.'

Chase moved out of the way, but Bea still had to brush past him to bend down to Chloe. He smelt really nice after his shower, and something tightened inside her as Chloe wound her arms around her neck and planted a smacking kiss on her cheek.

'Goodnight.' Absurdly flattered, Bea kissed her back.

She made as if to straighten, but Chloe's grip tightened. 'Another one!'

'No, we've all had a kiss now. Your uncle's kissed you, and you've kissed me.'

'You haven't kissed Uncle Chase,' Chloe pointed out with devastating logic, and stupidly, Bea felt herself colour.

'We're not going to bed,' she heard herself say. 'I mean, not yet.' God, that was even worse! 'That is we will go to bed, but not together,' she said firmly.

Chloe was doing her best to follow. 'Will you kiss him later, then?' she asked.

'Go to sleep, Chloe,' said her uncle calmly, and held the door open with what Bea was sure was mocking courtesy. 'Never get into an argument with a five-year-old,' he said, and, yes, that was *definitely* mockery in his voice!

Bea stalked past him, burningly conscious of what an idiot she must have sounded. What one earth had possessed her to start wittering on about going to bed, with or without him? It was all Chloe's fault for putting the idea of kissing Chase into her mind. It wasn't that she wanted to kiss him—God forbid! No, it was just that the thought had thrown her there for an instant.

Chloe could whistle for a story tomorrow, Bea decided.

Coming into the kitchen to make himself some coffee later that evening, Chase found Bea wearily drying a saucepan. Her hair swung forward to hide her face as she bent to put the lid away in a lower cupboard, and gleamed in the harsh overhead light. She was wearing a red dress with tiny little straps that left most of her shoulders bare, a distraction that had irritated Chase throughout supper when he had found it hard to concentrate on anything else.

Bea had to be the only cook they had ever had who dressed for dinner, he thought, exasperated. It was as if she was determined not to fit in. Chase could have told her she didn't need to put on a dress to look out of place. Everything she did made it obvious not only that she didn't belong, would never belong, but that she had absolutely no intention of belonging in the outback. If she hated it so much, why didn't she just leave? Chase wondered crossly.

But then she straightened as she saw him, pushing her hair behind her ears in what was already a familiar gesture, and he saw how tired she looked. She might be snooty, but she was a hard worker, he had to give her that.

'Why isn't Emily giving you a hand?' he asked roughly.

'She's not here as a cook.'

In spite of the fact that she had been furious when Emily had slipped out with Baz and the other stockmen the moment Chase had disappeared into his office, Bea felt obliged to defend her friend. It was a matter of loyalty, she told herself. Or habit.

Chase frowned. *She* wasn't there as a governess, but it hadn't stopped her spending time with Chloe, he found himself thinking. Now guess who was going to have to help her?

Picking up a big pot, he began drying it crossly with a tea towel. 'Where is Emily, anyway? Or need I ask?'

'I think she's with Baz,' said Bea with restraint, although she wasn't sure why she was bothering to be careful. It wasn't as if Emily had made any effort to disguise her obsession.

'I hope she doesn't mind being the latest in a very long line.'

The dismissive note in his voice made Bea's hackles rise. 'Oh?' she said sweetly. 'I understood that it was you who was used to working your way through the long line!'

To her annoyance, Chase looked amused, rather than embarrassed, or guilty or defensive. Instead of the way he *ought* to have looked, in fact.

'Who told you that?' he asked.

'Chloe seems to think that being a cook here automatically confers me with the position of your girlfriend!'

'And you're basing all your assumptions on the word of a five-year-old?'

Bea's lips tightened. She hated the way Chase always made her feel stupid. 'Is it true?'

'That you're my girlfriend?' Chase lifted a mocking eyebrow. 'Don't you think you'd know if you were?'

'It might be such a horrible thought that I've blocked it out,' snapped Bea, but to her fury, he only laughed.

And that made him look disconcertingly attractive, which made her even crosser.

'I think Chloe might be thinking of Kirsty,' said Chase.

Kirsty? How very cute.

'Or possibly Sue,' he went on, still drying his pot. 'Or do I mean Sophie?'

Bea stared suspiciously at him. Was he pulling her leg?

'Or Sara?'

'I'm surprised you can remember the names of all of them,' she said, more than a little piqued.

'I can't,' said Chase, still with that unsettling glint in his eye that made it impossible to know whether to take him seriously or not. 'Do you have any idea how many English girls have come out to Calulla Downs over the past few years? They're all just like you and Emily, thrilled with the whole idea of the outback and even more thrilled with the idea of marrying a million acres.'

'*Not* like me then!' said Bea, ruffling up immediately. 'I've felt lots of things since I arrived yesterday, but thrilled is not one of them!'

'Like Emily, then,' amended Chase. 'I could tell as soon as I saw her that she was going to be like all the others. She thinks it's all going to be so romantic, doesn't she? They all think that. They think they're going to ride around on horses, and lend a hand with mustering every now and then, and most of all, they think they're going to land themselves a guy with an Akubra and a property half the size of England that they can write home and boast about.'

Exactly what Emily had thought, in fact.

'Why not get an Australian girl to cook if we're such a terrible problem for you?'

'Easier said than done,' said Chase. 'Most Australian girls have got a more realistic idea of the outback, for a start. They know how hard life can be out here, and how lonely sometimes. It takes nearly two hours to drive to the nearest pub, and that's not exactly buzzing. If you're looking for night life, this isn't the place to come.'

'No kidding,' said Bea glumly, looking at the tea towel in her hand. Half past nine. She could be tucked up in a bar, right now, or at a movie, or planning a party. And instead she was washing dishes a hundred miles from anywhere.

'English girls are so bound up in their romantic ideas that they don't think about things

like that,' Chase went on as he reached for another pot. 'And as soon as they clapped eyes
on Nick, that was it. He's not just the eldest
son, he looks the part, and they'd all have a
little fantasy about being the next Mrs
Sutherland.'

'No doubt Nick was just fighting them all
off!' said Bea sarcastically.

'Oh, it had its advantages for him, all right.
It was worse for us. The quality of the food
would go down dramatically as the girl in question realised that Nick wasn't serious, then
we'd have tears, and the next thing, she'd have
left and then another one would have taken her
place.'

'It must have been a great relief for you when
Nick got married,' commented Bea drily.

'It might be a relief for Nick, but not much
else has changed. The girls still come, but now
if they want to be Mrs Sutherland there's only
one option...'

'They fall in love with *you?*' She stared at
him with unflattering incredulity.

'Who said anything about love?' said Chase
with a slight edge.

'So now you're the one who has to beat off
hordes of eager women?' Bea hoped that she
sounded suitably amused, as if she couldn't

care less about all those girls throwing themselves at him.

Hold on, that 'as if' wasn't right and, come to think of it, 'sounded' wasn't that convincing, either. Bea backtracked mentally…she *was* amused because she *couldn't* care less. Yes, that was better. No 'as if' about it.

Anyway, it looked as if Chase had got the right message. He was looking quite nettled, she noticed smugly.

'It's not always a question of beating them off,' he said.

Bea's smugness vanished abruptly. 'You sleep with them?' she said, and then winced inwardly at the note of outraged missionary in her voice. Of *course* he slept with them! What did she think, that he was saving himself for the right woman?

Chase raised an eyebrow. It was his turn to be amused now. 'Only the pretty ones,' he said.

Bea turned away and wrung out the cloth she had been using to wipe down the surfaces with unnecessary vigour. 'How discriminating of you!' she said tartly. 'How long do you give them before you dump them? A month? Six weeks?'

'It's not a question of dumping anybody. I've always made it clear that I've got no intention of marrying someone who'd be bored stiff before a year was out. It's been bad enough for Nick with Georgie, and she grew up on a station and should have known what she was getting into when she married him.'

Chase hung his damp tea towel over a cupboard door. 'No, I'm not tying myself to an unsuitable woman. I like a lot of the girls who come here. Most of them are good fun. It's not as if I've taken a vow of celibacy, or any of them are unwilling, so we have a good time while they're here and then they go. Six weeks is usually more than enough for them to realise not only that I'm not going to come through with a ring, but that they're not really cut out for the outback after all.'

'It must be a disappointment to you this time, then. Emily isn't the slightest bit interested in you!'

'No, life has been a lot easier since Baz arrived,' Chase agreed infuriatingly. 'Of course, he doesn't come with a property attached, so he tends to have better luck with the romantics like Emily. It's a pity he's leaving,' he went on, leaning back against the worktop and folding his arms. 'We'll have to make sure we get someone just as handsome to replace him.'

Bea was outraged at his cynical attitude. 'I hope Baz is leaving soon,' she said tight-lipped.

'In a couple of weeks. Why?'

'Because then Emily will want to leave too, and we can go back to Sydney. I hate to break with tradition,' she went on sarcastically, 'but I can tell you now that I have absolutely no intention of sleeping with you, falling in love with you or wanting to marry you!'

'Now that sounds like a challenge.' Chase straightened and walked across the kitchen to Bea, who found herself backing into the corner. He put one arm on either side of her, not touching her but effectively pinning her against the units. '*Is* it a challenge?' he asked softly.

Bea's heart was pounding. He was very close. She could see the lines fanning out from his eyes, the rough, masculine texture of his skin, the cool set of his mouth.

Oh, dear, she wished she hadn't noticed his mouth. Now she couldn't drag her eyes away from it.

She knew that all she had to do was to push his arm away and step past him, but somehow she couldn't move. Moistening her lips surreptitiously, she managed, 'I'd call it a promise rather than a challenge,' but her voice was uneven and her knees felt ridiculously weak.

And she still couldn't take her eyes from his mouth.

Unfairly, Chase smiled. 'Let's see, shall we?' he said, and his mouth came down on hers.

Bea just had time to brace herself for a hard, ruthless kiss which never came. Instead his mouth was warm and tantalising and so shockingly persuasive that the breath caught in her throat, parting her lips beneath his even as she closed her eyes against a startling jolt of response.

Before she quite knew how it had happened, she was kissing him back, and when Chase pulled her into his arms, she didn't even resist. His body was hard and exciting, and her hands slid over his shoulders as if they had a mind and a will of their own. More than she had, anyway. Bea's bones were dissolving, her head spinning, any will she had once had lost to the wicked excitement of his kiss, to the taste of his mouth and the strength of his hand sliding up her spine.

When Chase's lips left hers at last, Bea gasped with a mixture of protest and pleasure, only to shiver as they travelled deliciously along her jaw to the lobe of her ear.

'That was definitely a challenge,' he murmured, nibbling it gently, 'and what's more, I think I might accept it.'

Still drifting in the shivery excitement of his kiss, it took Bea a few seconds to assimilate this. The languid smile was wiped from her face as she realised what he had said, and she jerked herself out of his arms, her mind reeling.

What was she *doing?* Well, she knew what she had been doing, but not why. How on earth had she ended up kissing Chase Sutherland? She didn't even like the man...although who would have guessed that someone so brusque and businesslike could kiss like that?

Bea wrenched her drifting mind back to reality and pulled herself together with a huge effort. Great kisser he might be, but she certainly wasn't planning on falling into his arms like all of her predecessors. Well, not again, anyway.

'I wouldn't,' she said unsteadily. 'You'll lose.'

'Maybe, but it might be fun trying,' said Chase, and he smiled one of those smiles that had such an alarming effect on Bea's legs. 'Want some coffee?'

'What?'

Thrown as much by the smile as by the complete change of subject, Bea stared at him as he filled the kettle, clicked it on, and resumed his position leaning back against the units as if absolutely nothing had happened.

'I could make you some tea if you prefer,' he offered.

'Nothing, thank you,' said Bea stiffly.

She was still tingling from that kiss, and wondered if she was in shock. She certainly felt very odd. Almost like flinging herself back into his arms and begging him to kiss her again. Which must mean that she was unhinged. Or coming down with a very nasty virus.

'I think I'll go to bed,' she said. 'Alone,' she added, just in case he thought that she was inviting him along too. The worst thing was that she wouldn't be able to blame him if he *did* think that, not after the way she had melted into him and kissed him back.

Chase's eyes rested on her face, light, amused, unsettling as hell. 'Suit yourself,' was all he said as he turned away to make his coffee.

Now look what she had done! Bea tossed and turned irritably in her bed. She was exhausted, but she couldn't sleep. How could she sleep after being kissed like that?

If only it hadn't felt quite so good. Why couldn't Chase go in for wet, slobbery kisses, or be one of those guys who set about your mouth as if they were vacuuming it? Then she wouldn't be lying awake like this, wondering about all those other girls he had kissed in the same kitchen, girls who would know what else he might be surprisingly good at...

Bea rolled over and punched her pillow into shape. It wasn't that she was interested in the idea of sleeping with Chase. She wasn't. Not in the slightest. *Especially* not knowing that for him she was just a challenge.

It was just that now that she had started to think about it, she couldn't *stop* thinking about what it might be like.

The more Bea thought about it, the more she liked the idea that she might be going down with a virus. It would explain the dizziness and the trembling legs and the fact that she hadn't been thinking clearly. So, really, she wasn't responsible for kissing Chase back like that at all. She wasn't attracted to him at all, she was just sick.

Oh, yes, it was definitely a virus.

Bea had just dropped off to sleep at last when Emily came in and woke her up. 'Are you asleep?'

'Yes,' mumbled Bea.

'I just had to tell you...I'm in love!'

'Great.' Bea turned over to bury her face in her pillow.

'Baz is everything I've always wanted!' Oblivious to Bea's attempts to go back to sleep, Emily chattered on about Baz as she undressed and jumped into bed. 'I'm sorry I had to leave you with that grumpy Chase all evening, though,' she went on as an obvious after-thought. 'Was it really boring?'

Bea was lying with her back turned pointedly to Emily, but at that her eyes snapped open and she stared unseeingly at the wall. Chase, bor-ing? She thought about the feel of his hands, the touch of his lips, the way he had smiled against her mouth as he pulled her closer, the glint in his eyes as he had let her go.

'No,' was all she said.

'Oh, good.' Emily snuggled down into bed and switched off the light. 'Then you won't mind if I spend tomorrow night with Baz again, will you?'

Breakfast was at five thirty the next morning, which meant that Bea got a whole half hour extra in bed. Not that it made much difference. It was still dark, and still a completely unnat-ural time to wake up as far as Bea was concerned. When the alarm clock went off, she had to force herself to throw back the covers and stumble into her clothes.

It was still cold, too.

Bea's eye fell on the sweatshirt hanging over the back of the chair where she had left it yesterday when the sun was beating down outside and she hadn't been able to imagine ever being cold again. Chase's sweatshirt. The sight of it was enough to bring back the memory of that kiss the previous evening in a rush that did more than the chill night air to wake her up.

She hesitated for a moment, and then pulled it over her head, tugging it down crossly as she tried to ignore the tiny shiver of familiarity at the scent of him that still lingered in the fabric. She was not going to freeze to death just because Chase had kissed her.

In fact, she wasn't going to dignify what had happened with any comment at all. The last thing she wanted was for Chase to imagine that she had spent half the night reliving the entire experience, even if she had. No, far better to just ignore the whole topic.

It was a good decision, but it didn't stop Bea's heart giving a tiny jerk when Chase walked into the kitchen. Quickly, she lifted her chin and turned her head away, although she needn't have bothered. It was pretty obvious that Chase had decided to ignore the entire issue too.

He was talking about some e-mail he had had from Nick, something about visitors, and making beds, but Bea wasn't listening. She was considering the possibility that perhaps Chase wasn't ignoring the kiss at all. Perhaps he had kissed so many cooks in the kitchen that she had just blurred into the memory of all those others.

Bea stabbed at the steaks under the grill, distinctly disgruntled at the thought. OK, so she had wanted to ignore the fact that they had kissed in this very room the night before, but not if it meant Chase simply wiping the whole incident from his mind! It was his fault, after all. She might have kissed him back, but he had kissed her first. By rights, he should be on his knees with a grovelling apology.

For a moment, Bea let herself imagine it. It would be a perfect opportunity for her to pretend that she couldn't understand what he was making such a fuss about, and that she was the one who had forgotten all about it. 'Kiss? What kiss?' she would say, and then she might even laugh. 'You don't really call that a *kiss*, do you?'

She could picture her own expression of amused superiority perfectly. Chase was the trouble. Try as she might, she just couldn't imagine him on his knees, grovelling, or making a fuss about anything.

Shame.

'So is that OK with you?'

Chase's voice broke into her thoughts, and she looked up from the grill. 'What?'

He sighed. 'Have you heard a word I've been saying, Bea?'

'Something about an e-mail?' she tried.

Chase controlled his irritation with an effort and started again. 'Nick e-mailed me last night. He does all the arrangements for Georgie's paying guests, and he'd forgotten to remind me that another lot are due to arrive today. Two couples, apparently, so there'll be four more for supper. Can you cope with that?'

'Of course I can cope,' said Bea, offended.

'At least they're driving themselves, so they won't need to be picked up, but I could have done without them today,' Chase went on. 'I want to check the bores out at Kilungra, and we'll be gone all day. Which reminds me, can you put together some sandwiches? Oh, and something for smoko.'

'Oh, sure, it's not as if I've got anything else to do, just cook breakfast for nine, plan supper for thirteen and now you want sandwiches and biscuits as well!'

'You just said you could cope.'

'I can cope,' said Bea. 'I just appreciate a bit of notice.'

Chase was unmoved. 'You can do the sandwiches while we're having breakfast,' he said.

Bea was glad to see the back of them for the day. She sent them off with a big packet of sandwiches made with leftover roast, and the last of the rock cakes, which meant that she would have to make something else for the guests when they arrived. In spite of her grumbling, she even had time to offer to make up a Thermos of tea, but Chase shook his head.

'We'll just boil up a billy,' he said, and Bea wasn't about to give him the satisfaction of asking what *that* meant.

As soon as he had gone, though, the homestead felt strangely empty. Even when Chloe, and later Emily, appeared, Bea couldn't shake off the feeling of absence, and she kept listening out for the sound of his boots on the veranda steps, or the tell-tale creak of the screen door.

It wasn't that she was missing him, of course. It just seemed like a long day without the men coming back for smoko or lunch, and the three girls felt lost and a bit silly sitting at one end of the big table.

And it wasn't as if she didn't have anything to do. Bea hardly drew breath all day. She ran around making beds, cleaning bedrooms, picking flowers, knocking up a cake and a supply of flapjacks, feeding chickens and dogs, sweeping the veranda, and preparing the meal for that night. Chloe and Emily offered occasional help and advice, but they had identically low boredom thresholds, and in the end Bea found it easier to do most things herself.

The paying guests arrived in the late afternoon. All Americans, they were initially thrown to be greeted at the archetypal Australian homestead by the unmistakably English Bea, but by the time she had shown them to their rooms and given them tea on the veranda, they were ready to be charmed by everything. They told Bea that they were fulfilling a lifelong dream to drive around Australia, but that this was the first time they had ventured into the outback.

'I was nervous about camping,' Joan confided with a guilty laugh. 'Ben laughs at me about it, but you hear so much about spiders and snakes in the outback, don't you?'

Bea gulped. She hadn't thought about spiders, let alone snakes. Why hadn't she remembered them when she was trying to convince Emily that she didn't want to come?

'Then a friend of a friend who knows Georgie Grainger recommended Calulla Downs. It sounded just what we wanted, to stop travelling for a few days and share in life on a cattle station but in comfort, and I must say everything is even better than we expected.' Joan beamed. 'It's certainly worth that long drive. We have plenty of isolated ranches in the States, but this place is something else again, isn't it?'

'It certainly is,' said Bea drily, marvelling that anyone would actually pay to come out there.

Supper that night was a noisy, jolly affair with so many people around the table. The Americans were as chatty as Emily, and so pleased to be there that Chase didn't have to do much to keep the conversation going.

It meant that he was able to watch Bea at the other end of the table instead. She wasn't *that* pretty, he told himself. She had a fine-boned face, with strong features and clear skin that flushed easily, but the most distinctive thing about her was those strange golden eyes.

There was something odd about her hair too. Chase frowned slightly, trying to work out what it was, but then shrugged mentally and pushed the problem aside. She was resting her chin on one palm, smiling at something Joan's husband saying to her, and Chase marvelled again at how a smile transformed her face, lighting it up in a way that made his heart tighten strangely.

She was dressed up as usual, still pretending that she was in Sydney, no doubt, but it was a different dress tonight, something cream and classy with a demure neckline. Chase was glad of it. He had spent most of the day trying to forget how she had felt in the red dress the night before.

His palms felt twitchy, as if he could still feel the silky material slipping over her body beneath his hands, and he swallowed. She looked so cool, but last night her mouth had been warm and soft, and she had felt so good...

It had been a mistake, Chase told himself firmly. He shouldn't have kissed her, but something about her had got under his skin in a way none of the other girls he had known had. He didn't want Bea going the same way as them. They needed a cook at Calulla Downs and, with

Nick away, he couldn't afford the time to re-place her. If Bea threw down any more chal-lenges like the one last night, he would ignore them.

Well, he would try.

'Here.' Chase handed Bea a mug of coffee and sat down beside her in one of the wicker chairs.

'Thanks.'

Bea wasn't quite sure what was going on. After their long drive, the guests had opted for an early night, but Chase had caught Emily just as she and Baz were hoping that they could do the same. He had insisted that she help Bea with the washing up, and had stood over them until the kitchen was spotless, much to Emily's disgust. She had spent most of her time rolling her eyes behind his back until Bea wished that she had been left to do it all by herself after all.

At last, Chase had let Emily leave, and then he had announced gruffly that he would bring Bea coffee on the veranda if she wanted to go and sit down.

It was still relatively early and, in spite of the busy day, Bea wasn't tired enough to go to bed. Nor could she admit that she was nervous about being alone with him, even to herself. So she took the mug Chase handed her and cradled her hands around it, trying to forget just what they had been doing when they had found themselves alone together the night before.

'What's brought all this on?' she asked.

'I thought I owed you a cup of coffee at least,' said Chase. 'Joan and the others have been telling me how impressed they were with the welcome you gave them today. They really liked the bush flowers in their rooms and the tea on the veranda. I don't think any of our other guests have been treated as well.'

He glanced at Bea. 'It could have been awkward with me being out all day, and not here to welcome them, but it's obvious that they're going to be happy with everything because of you. I guess I just wanted to say thank you. I know how hard you must have worked all day.'

Bea shifted uncomfortably, uncertain like most people as to how to deal with gratitude. 'I always wanted to have my own hotel,' she said as lightly as she could. 'Think of it as me living out my fantasy!'

'That's your fantasy?' said Chase incredulously.

It did sound a bit tame, Bea had to admit. 'Well, one of them,' she said.

'What are the others?'

It was dark on the veranda, and the night air was blissfully cool. Below, the blue light crackled as flying bugs blundered into its trap, but otherwise it was absolutely quiet. Just the kind of background to start blurting out things that you would regret the next morning.

'They're private,' said Bea.

Chase's smile gleamed through the darkness. 'Very sensible,' he commented in a dry voice.

'That's me, sensible Bea,' said Bea with an edge of bitterness. *You're so sensible, Bea,* Phil had used to sigh. *You don't know how to let yourself go.*

'You surprise me,' said Chase honestly. 'Sensible is the last word I'd use to describe you.'

Bea wasn't sure whether to be pleased or offended. She turned her head to look at him. 'Why not?'

He hadn't been expecting that, and had to think for a moment. 'Well, you don't wear sensible shoes,' he said, and she forgot any thought of being offended and laughed instead.

'Why, Mr Sutherland, that's the nicest thing you've ever said to me!'

'You're welcome,' said Chase, and because she looked so different when she was smiling, he smiled back.

As soon as their eyes met, Bea knew that smiling was a mistake. It changed something in the air, and made the dark veranda intimate, as if they were friends and not two people with completely different lives who didn't even like each other very much.

Biting her lip, she looked quickly away and stared out into the darkness with a kind of desperation. Now was absolutely *not* the time to start remembering that she hadn't disliked the way he had kissed her!

There was a short, strained silence, broken only by the regular zap and crackle of the blue light, and eventually by Chase clearing his throat.

'Why aren't you running a hotel now, if that's what you want?' he asked, sounding reassuringly like someone who had found the silence as uncomfortable as she had.

'Money,' said Bea, grateful to him for the change of subject. 'I haven't got any capital, and at the current rate, I never will have. Anyway, the kind of hotel I'd always imagined would be out in the country somewhere, and as you know, I'm not a country girl. You've got to be realistic about these things. I'd go mad if I lived in a place like this the whole time. I need to be in a city, the bigger and busier the better.'

No harm in reminding Chase that she at least wasn't in the running for the coveted position of his wife.

'Doing what?' he asked. 'Or is that one of your private fantasies?'

'I want to set up my own business,' said Bea. 'I've planned it all. I'm going to specialise in catering for social events like PR launches or smart parties. If you want to make a splash nowadays you've got to provide more than a bowl of nuts and a warm glass of white wine. The food can set the tone of the whole occasion. I can do clever canapés, new twists on finger food, imaginative nibbles...you know the kind of thing.'

'No,' said Chase, 'but I'll take your word for it.'

'I'll still need a loan, of course,' she went on, warming to her theme, 'but not nearly as much as I would need if I wanted to take over a hotel. It might take a little time to build the business up and make contacts, but I know I can do it,' she added determinedly.

Chase wasn't so sure. He'd seen enough of her to know that she was organised and efficient and a hard worker, but that mouth of hers gave her away. It wasn't nearly ruthless enough to belong to a successful businesswoman.

'Is there enough call for that kind of thing in Sydney?' he asked.

'Oh, yes, there's always something happening in Sydney. They have the best parties there.' Bea sighed nostalgically. 'I wish I could stay, but my visa runs out soon, and I'll have to go back to London.'

To London. To Phil and her family and all those humiliating memories.

Chase heard her voice change. 'You don't sound very enthusiastic about it.'

'No.'

'Don't you like London?'

Once, she had loved it. 'It's not that. It's just the thought of leaving Australia and never seeing Sydney again.'

'Come back, if that's the way you feel.'

'I can't afford it, especially not if I'm going to set myself up in business, and even if I could, I'd be too old for a work permit by the time I got here. If I was a brain surgeon or something useful, I'd be able to apply to emigrate, but as it is being able to make miniature Thai crab cakes or caper flower garnishes doesn't count for very much.'

Bea contemplated her future glumly for a moment, and then squared her shoulders. There was no point in whingeing. That was the way things were, and she was just going to have to get on with it.

'Anyway, what about you?' she asked, turning to him, determinedly cheerful. 'What's your fantasy?'

Chase raised an eyebrow. 'Do we know each other well enough for me to tell you that?'

'I'm talking about making a living,' said Bea with a frosty look. As if he didn't know perfectly well what she had meant. 'Haven't you ever wanted to go to a city?'

'You think I've never been beyond Mackinnon?' said Chase drily. 'I've been to plenty of cities.'

'I meant to work.'

He shrugged. 'I worked in London for a bit when I was travelling, but it wasn't my kind of place. I like to be able to see the horizon.'

'But don't you ever get bored? It's all so...so empty!'

'That depends what you're looking for,' said Chase.

'What about shops and bars and restaurants and cinemas and art galleries and museums and concerts...?'

'No, we don't do those,' he said, unfazed. 'We just do space and stillness and silence. And the bush. You never get bored of the bush.'

That's what he thought. Bea glanced at him. 'Looks like we're incompatible,' she said.

'Looks that way,' Chase agreed, although he didn't sound very bothered by the fact. 'Lucky you don't want to marry me, isn't it?'

'Very lucky,' said Bea crisply.

A little *too* crisply, perhaps.

CHAPTER FIVE

By Saturday, Bea was starting to get used to getting up in the dark and cooking steak and eggs at a time when most normal people were still asleep. Getting used to it didn't mean that she was enjoying it, though. She told herself that the experience would prove useful in another life, although it was difficult to imagine what that life might be.

It was increasingly hard, in fact, to imagine anything other than being at Calulla Downs. Her life in Sydney already seemed to belong to someone else altogether, while London was unimaginably distant.

Wryly, she remembered telling Emily how boring it would be in the outback. She never had any time to be bored, just as Chase had forecast that first evening. She was working harder than she ever had before. Exhausted by her passionate encounters with Baz, Emily had yet to wake before eight, by which time Bea felt as if she had been up for half a day, cooking breakfast, baking for smoko and tidying up the kitchen while Chloe ate hers, listening with half an ear to her chatter.

Together, they would take the scraps down to the chooks and collect the eggs. The trip across the yard and down a short, dusty track was the furthest Bea had been from the homestead. She liked the light then, before the sun started to glare and dazzle, and while the air was still flushed with the memory of dawn, and the birds squawked and wheeled above the trees.

Sometimes they would come across a wallaby on the track. It would freeze when it saw them, bounding off into the bush at the last minute as they approached. The mere sight of a wallaby or a kangaroo was so Australian that it always gave Bea a little thrill, but Chloe was less impressed.

'Chase says they're a pest,' she informed Bea. 'We should call the roo shooter.'

'Oh, but they're so pretty!'

Chase rolled his eyes when this conversation was reported to him by Chloe. 'I don't care what they look like, they're still pests! I need the grass for my cattle.'

At least the Americans tourists were on Bea's side. They were having a wonderful time. Chase took them out in his big four-wheel drive to show them some of the station, and another day they all got on horses to help muster the near paddocks.

'You should have come with us,' Joan enthused to Bea at dinner one evening when they got back from a drive along the creek. Bea had given them a packed lunch, and they were full of excitement when they came back. 'It's so beautiful!'

'The bush isn't Bea's thing,' said Chase before she could answer. There was an odd edge to his voice. 'She likes cities, don't you, Bea?'

'Yes, I'm an urban chick,' she agreed brightly. 'Give me a café and a newspaper and a crowd of people to watch, and I'm happy.'

But the truth was that she wasn't missing the city nearly as much as she had expected. She liked the cooking, she liked picking lemons straight off the tree, she liked the cool, quiet homestead and sitting around the big table every evening.

And then there was Chase.

Every evening, Emily disappeared off with Baz, and it wasn't long before she was spending the entire night in the stockmen's quarters. It meant that Bea had a room to herself, and although she could have gone there after supper, it seemed unsociable to leave Chase to entertain the guests on his own. So Bea stayed, and somehow they had fallen into a routine of sitting on in the dark after the others had gone to bed.

After a rocky start, they knew where they were with each other. Now that they had established that they were incompatible, it was easier to talk. They both knew that the other was not what they wanted, so they could relax.

Bea hardly ever thought about that kiss now. Only sometimes, when their eyes met across the table, or when she looked at his mouth, or watched his hands brushing the dust off his hat.

Only every now and then.

'Oh, but you must see more of the outback since you're here,' Joan was saying, unconvinced by Bea's assurance that she wasn't interested. 'You'll fall in love with it!'

'Bea doesn't do falling in love either,' said Chase.

There was a tiny, awkward silence.

Bea smiled as if he had made a joke. 'I'm leaving soon, anyway,' she said. 'There's no point in me falling in love now.'

It was probably just as well she was going, Chase thought. He was glad that she had reminded him. He was getting too used to coming home and finding her there.

She had seemed so uptight at first, but sometimes she would forget that she was supposed to be practical and efficient, and she would relax and smile. Sometimes Chase wished she wouldn't. It made it harder to forget what it had been like to kiss her, how warm and good she had felt in his arms.

He watched her now, laughing with Joan, her face all lit up and that mouth as disturbing as ever. Her hair curved straight and gleaming beneath her chin. When she was unsure, she would tuck it behind her ears, but at other times it swung around her face and she would shake it back in a gesture that never failed to dry the breath in his throat.

She wasn't his type, of course. She was too much of a city girl, too sharp and too strained. She cared too much about appearances and every time he turned round she seemed to have a different outfit on. She certainly wasn't interested in *him*.

It was just that she was a hard worker, Chase told himself. A hard worker and a great cook. If it hadn't been for her, the Americans' visit would have been a disaster. He hadn't had time to look after them properly but Bea had made sure that everyone was comfortable. Chloe was happy, too—no thanks to that Emily, who as far as Chase could make out lazed around all day while Bea did all the work.

So while Bea still wasn't his type, he found himself looking forward to coming home at the end of the day. Too often in the past, the atmosphere when he walked up the veranda steps had been fraught with tension. Nick and Georgie were rowing, or the latest cook, in love with Baz, or disappointed in him, was tearful.

There was none of that with Bea. Chase liked sitting on the veranda with her when the Americans had gone to bed. He could talk to her in the darkness without her mentally choosing a wedding dress, and if once or twice he thought about how close she was, and how easy it would be to reach out and kiss her again, well, that didn't mean anything.

It didn't mean that he would miss her when she went back to the city. She was just another temporary cook.

The Americans left the following Saturday, with many kisses and promises to stay in touch. The homestead seemed very quiet after they had gone. When Chase came back at five o'clock, he found Bea giving Chloe her supper.

'Where's Emily?' he asked, hanging up his hat with a frown.

'She's gone with Baz and the others into the pub in town.'

'Didn't you want to go?'

Bea was washing up a saucepan. 'Someone's got to keep an eye on Chloe,' she said mildly.

'Why?' said Chloe.

Chase scowled. 'You should have told me. I would have come home earlier. I always let the boys go off early on a Saturday.'

'It doesn't matter.' Bea wiped her hands on a tea towel. 'I don't really fancy driving for a couple of hours along a dirt road to go to a noisy pub, drink myself stupid and then drive all the way back again.'

You know your trouble, Bea? Emily had said. *You've got no sense of adventure. You should relax, learn to live a little.*

She smiled crookedly. 'Emily says I'm being boring.'

'What does Emily know?' Chase bristled. 'As far as I can see, she hasn't lifted a finger all week, except to deprive Baz of sleep. He's not exactly chatty at the best of times, but he's been walking round like a zombie since you two arrived. He used to be a good stockman, but he's useless to me at the moment. It'll be a relief when he leaves.'

'I'd forgotten he was going,' said Bea slowly.

'I thought you were counting the days,' said Chase, trying and failing to keep the note of jealousy from his voice.

She *had* said that, Bea remembered. She had told Chase that she couldn't wait to go back to the city. It felt like a lifetime ago.

'Emily's going to be upset,' she said, as if excusing herself. 'She's absolutely besotted with Baz.'

Personally, she couldn't see the attraction. Baz was handsome, sure, but he hardly ever opened his mouth. You couldn't sit and talk to him the way you could with someone like Chase, say.

Just for an example.

'Stop worrying about Emily,' Chase ordered roughly. 'She can look after herself.'

'I'm not worrying,' lied Bea. 'I'm just tired.'

'Well, tomorrow's your day off. You can have a lie-in. Nobody turns up for breakfast, and we just have a barbecue in the evening, so you won't have to do any cooking.'

'What about Chloe?' asked Bea, glancing at the little girl who was following their conversation with intense interest.

'I'll look after Chloe,' said Chase. 'You do what you want.'

'Great,' she said, but she couldn't help wondering what on earth she was going to do with herself all day. She wouldn't be able to buy the Sunday papers and sit reading them. There were no markets to potter round out here, no cafés where she could have a long, lazy breakfast, no galleries to visit, or cinemas showing double bills. There wasn't even a friend to ring up and suggest that they spent the day together, doing nothing.

There was Chase, of course, but he wasn't really a friend, was he? He was her employer, to all intents and purposes, and he hadn't shown any interest in spending the day with her.

Not that she wanted him to, of course.

Perversely, Bea woke without the alarm at five the next morning. When she saw what time it was, she willed herself to go back to sleep, but it was hopeless, and it was only as matter of principle that she made herself lie there until six.

Thoroughly awake by then, she decided to go and make herself a cup of tea. She would take it back to bed, and that would be her treat.

Tea in bed? Was that the best she could do? Bea shook her head and threw back the bedcovers.

It was just light as she made her way along the corridor to the kitchen, the wood cool beneath her bare feet. She could hear the counterpoint of Chase's deep voice with Chloe's light one, and she hesitated in the doorway, suddenly shy.

'Bea!' cried Chloe, spotting her, and Chase turned from the sink where he was filling the kettle to see Bea standing there, bare-legged and tousled in a baggy T-shirt. It didn't take much stretch of the imagination to guess that she wore absolutely nothing underneath.

Chase's throat tightened and he swallowed with some difficulty. 'You want to be careful wandering around in bare feet,' he said, hoping that she wouldn't notice how odd his voice sounded.

'Why?' That was Chloe, of course.

'Spiders,' he said briefly. 'You don't want to tread on a redback.'

Bea leapt onto a chair, tucking her legs up beneath her, and stared down at the floor in horror as if expecting to see it heaving with creepy-crawlies. Her expression was so apprehensive that Chase couldn't help laughing, and somehow the awkward moment when all he could think about was her warm, naked body had passed.

'Chloe will go and get your shoes for you, won't you, Chloe?'

Chloe ran off obligingly and the two of them were left alone in the kitchen. Chase turned his attention firmly back to the kettle.

'I keep forgetting about things like spiders,' said Bea. 'Just when you think you're starting to get used to it, you realise you're in a foreign country.'

'They're not too much of a problem. You just have to be careful.'

When he switched the kettle on, the click sounded very loud in the silence.

'I thought you were having a lie-in,' he said after a moment.

'I tried,' said Bea. 'I never thought I'd see the day when it felt lazy to be lying in bed at six in the morning!'

'You must be adapting to the outback.'

'I must be.'

Bea couldn't look at Chase. Last night had been bad enough, when the easy atmosphere on the veranda had evaporated in the conscious-ness that the two of them were utterly alone apart from Chloe sleeping inside. They would

talk stiltedly for a while, and then the conversation would dry up without warning, leaving
them marooned in an ever-tightening silence. In
the end, Bea had muttered something about being tired and had escaped to her room.

She had thought it would be easier in the
daylight, but somehow it wasn't.

'Here you are!' Chloe came running back
with Bea's sandals, and thrust them into her
hand.

'Thank you, sweetheart.'

Bea slipped the shoes on, but it didn't stop
her feeling burningly conscious of her naked-
ness beneath her T-shirt. Why hadn't she got
dressed before she came along to the kitchen?

'Your hair,' said Chase suddenly.

'What about it?'

'It's been bothering me all week, and I've
just realised why. It's always curly in the morn-
ings, and straight in the evenings.'

Involuntarily, Bea's hand went to her hair. 'I
haven't washed it yet.'

'It goes straight when you wash it?'

Chloe cast him a pitying look. 'She dries it
with a *hair-dryer,*' she said, rolling her eyes at
his ignorance.

'What, every day?'

A flush rose in Bea's cheeks. 'Yes.'

There was a pause. 'Why?' said Chase eventually, unable to think of anything else to say. He sounded just like Chloe, he realised ruefully.

'Because I hate it like this.' Bea plucked resentfully at her wild brown curls. 'It's bad enough at home, but when it's hot like this it goes even kinkier.'

'I like it,' he said, considering her. 'You should leave it. Think how much time you'd save every day.'

'I can't carry off the natural look,' said Bea, on the defensive. She hated any discussion of her horrible hair. 'I like to keep my hair and my life under control.'

'Control freak,' said Chase as he made a pot of tea.

'That's what Emily says,' she said glumly. 'She's always telling me I should learn to live dangerously.'

Chase put the teapot down on the table, but he was careful not to come to close to her. 'Start by not washing your hair on Sundays,' he suggested lightly.

'I like it when it's curly,' announced Chloe. 'Don't make it straight today, Bea.'

'Come riding with us instead.' The offer was out before Chase quite knew what he was saying. Just what he needed, a whole day of trying not to let Bea distract him! Why hadn't he kept his mouth shut?

Chloe was thrilled at the idea. 'Oh, yes, come with us, Bea!'

'I don't know how to ride, Chloe.'

She had given him the perfect let-out. Instead of taking it, Chase heard himself offering to find her a quiet horse.

'It's easy,' Chloe assured her. 'Isn't it, Uncle Chase?'

'We'll take it slowly,' he promised, pouring out two mugs of tea.

Bea couldn't take her eyes from his fingers curled around the teapot handle. The sight of them did something funny to her insides. Last night had been awkward enough. How would she manage a whole day in his company?

Chloe was jumping up and down by Bea's chair. 'Say you'll come, Bea!'

Chase could see Bea chewing her lip indecisively. 'Maybe Bea wants to have some time to herself,' he suggested.

That would be the safe option, Bea thought, but she was getting a bit sick of the safe option. Maybe Emily was right and it was time she lived a little. A day with a five-year-old and a horse would hardly qualify her for membership in the extreme sports club, after all. They weren't suggesting that she jumped out of plane or threw herself off a cliff. It would just be her and Chloe.

And Chase.

Even she couldn't be pathetic enough to be nervous about that, could she?

'No, I'd like to come,' she said, making up her mind. 'If I leave my hair as well, this will really be my chance to live dangerously!'

She almost lost her nerve when she saw the size of the horse Chase had saddled for her. Suddenly the idea of a bungee jump didn't look so bad.

'How am I going to get up there?'

'Put your foot in the stirrup,' said Chase, holding it for her. He gave her the reins to hold in one hand and made her hang onto the saddle with the other, and before Bea had time to panic, he had boosted her up into the saddle.

Bea swallowed. It looked a long way down to the ground. 'Don't let him run away with me,' she said nervously.

'I thought you wanted to live dangerously?'

He was grinning up at her, his eyes beneath his hat light with amusement, and the breath clogged in Bea's throat as she looked down into his face, suddenly very glad of the sunglasses that hid her expression.

'Not that dangerously,' she managed with difficulty.

'Don't worry.' Chase slapped the horse's neck affectionately. 'Old Duke here won't go faster than a walk, and even if he went wild and broke into a trot, I've got you.' He showed her the leading rein he held in his hand.

'Well, please don't let me go,' said Bea, trying to make a joke of it, but somehow it came out all wrong, and Chase looked up at her.

'I won't,' he said.

Chloe was already on a fat little pony, looking quite at home. Chase settled his hat on his head and swung himself up onto an even bigger horse than Bea's. Emily would have appreciated the sight, thought Bea, trying not to think about the look in his eyes.

At first it took all her attention just staying on the swaying horse, but as soon as it became obvious that Duke was happy to plod along and not do anything alarming, Bea let herself relax a bit and even to look around her.

The sun was already high in the sky, but it was pleasantly shady under the trees along the creek. There had been no need for Chase to insist that she wore one of his old hats, she thought, remembering the sharp little argument they'd had when she proposed going out without one. He had won, of course, and now her hair was going to look even worse than usual.

Chloe was trotting confidently ahead. As she passed under a branch of a great ghost gum, a flock of cockatoos erupted into flight, screeching indignantly at the disturbance. Bea's gaze followed them as they wheeled and darted through the trees and, turning her head, she found Chase watching her.

Something about the way he smiled made her put up her chin. 'Don't tell me, you have to teach all your cooks to ride!'

He shook his head. 'You're the first.'

'I find that rather hard to believe,' she said as coolly as she could.

'It's the truth.'

Bea regarded him uncertainly, not sure whether he was joking or not. 'Why me, then?'

'Maybe I like the idea of you not being good at something,' he said. 'Maybe I like the idea that for once you won't know what you're doing. You're always so practical and competent in the homestead, but out here you're going to have to rely on Chloe and me. It wouldn't kill you to let someone else look after you for once.'

He was teasing…wasn't he? Bea stared at him, her heart beating uncomfortably, and then just when she had decided that he might be serious, he smiled. He was so clearly outlined against the bush, and his teeth were so white and his eyes so light that she felt suddenly giddy.

Wrenching her gaze away with an effort, she gripped the reins in her hands and stared resolutely between Duke's flickering ears. That disturbing lurch of her heart didn't mean anything. For a moment there she had felt suspended in time and space, but it had just been the heat and the light and the silence making her dizzy, playing tricks on her.

Nothing to do with Chase.

Nothing at all.

The bed of the creek was bone dry and littered with the bleached branches of fallen trees. Chase told Bea how it flooded in the wet season, but she couldn't imagine the churning water or the way the grass grew with the rain. She had grown so used to the brown, bare landscape that she exclaimed with surprise and pleasure when they came to a waterhole so deep that it survived the searing heat of summer.

'Fancy some tea?' Chase asked Bea, who was so thirsty by then that her face lit up as if he had offered her champagne.

Dismounting, Chase tied up his horse with Bea's and moved to help Chloe down. She was having none of it. 'I can do it!' she said stubbornly, kicking her feet out of the stirrups and slithering to the ground.

'What about you?' Chase smiled up at Bea, and her heart gave a breathless little somersault. 'Can you get off on your own?'

Bea would have given anything to have been able to manage by herself as Chloe had done but, short of a ladder, there was no way of getting down.

'I think I'd better have my lunch up here,' she said, and then Chase destroyed all her resolve by laughing.

'Put your hands on my shoulders,' he said, and held up his arms. Taking her by the waist, he lifted her down and set her on the ground.

Clumsy with sudden shyness, Bea stumbled against him. His body was strong and rock solid, and her mouth dried with lust. Even when she had pulled herself away with a muttered apology, she felt boneless and light-headed.

Too much sun, she told herself.

She sat on a warm, worn rock in the shade
and watched Chloe scrambling happily around
the waterhole. Behind her, the horses stood pa-
tiently, shaking their heads every now and then
against the flies. Their harness chinked softly
and they exchanged an occasional whicker,
while all around them the cicadas scraped and
sawed in a raucous symphony.

With quick, deft movements, Chase made a
fire among some stones, and fetched what
looked like a large can with a handle on top of
it from his saddle.

'What's that?' asked Bea as he set it over the
fire.

He looked up at her over his shoulder. 'How
long have you been in Australia?' he asked.

'Nearly a year.'

'And you've never had billy tea before?'

Oh, so *that* was a billy. Bea had often wondered. But the derisive note in Chase's voice
made her put up her chin. 'No, I'm glad to say
it's always been possible to pop out for a cappuccino wherever I've been before.'

'Right,' said Chase drily, and went back to
poking the fire with a stick.

Bea eyed him almost resentfully. It wasn't
her fault she hadn't grown up in the outback.
There was no point in her pretending that she

was anything other than a city girl. Chase didn't seem to realise how alien all this was to her. Emily might appreciate the startling light, and the hot, dry scent of the bush, but she was a girl who liked a pavement beneath her feet, and was used to grabbing a cab, not throwing herself on a horse.

Emily would love the idea of riding along a creek and drinking tea out of a billy. She would be thrilled by the sight of Chase, hunkered down by the fire, the brim of his hat pulled down over his eyes, looking utterly at home even without a checked shirt.

Bea's eyes rested on him, on the curve of his back, on the lean length of his thigh, on the line of his jaw, and heat flooded through her without warning. She had a terrible urge to go and crouch next to him and put her hand on his shoulder, to lean into him and breathe in the scent of his skin. To let him pull her down onto the ground and to hell with the dust and the dried leaves and even the insects if only he'd touch her...

Gulping, Bea tore her gaze away. If she wasn't careful, she'd end up like Emily, carried away by a fantasy that had no basis in reality. The reality was that she and Chase might as well come from different planets, and that she would be leaving soon in any case. So there was no point in even *thinking* about finding him attractive, was there?

Was there?

No, Bea answered herself firmly. None at all.

Chase was throwing some tea leaves into the billy and stirring it with a stick. He let it steep for a while, then poured the tea into a couple of battered enamel mugs and handed one to Bea. As she reached out for it, her fingers brushed his and she snatched her hand back without thinking.

If Chase had felt a similar jolt of electricity at the touch of her skin, he gave absolutely no sign of it. All he did was look exasperated. 'Careful!' he said, and offered her the mug again. 'Now, have you got it?' he demanded, much as he might to a child.

'Yes,' muttered Bea, humiliated. She took the mug very carefully, trying to avoid his fingers, and then, just when she thought she'd got herself under control, Chase sat down on the rock beside her, and all her senses jerked into a state of full alert.

Chase misunderstood her expression. 'Sorry it's not a cappuccino,' he said.

'It's fine,' said Bea, searching wildly for an excuse. 'A bit hot, that's all.'

She made a big deal of blowing on her tea, keeping her eyes firmly away from Chase's jean-clad thigh that was disturbingly close to her own, and took a cautious sip. To her surprise, it tasted more than fine, it tasted delicious.

It must be because she was so thirsty, Bea decided. It was nothing to do with being out here with the light and the gum trees and the drifting fragrance of the bush, or with the fact that Chase was sitting beside her, still and self-contained.

She was a girl who liked champagne and cocktails, or if it had to be tea, would insist on Lapsang Souchong. She wasn't a girl who would ever be happy with a few coarse tea leaves shoved into a tin can and stirred with a stick. So it had to be thirst that was making it taste so good.

In spite of herself, Bea's eyes slid sideways. Chase was leaning forward, drinking his tea, apparently absorbed in watching Chloe playing by the waterhole. His body was lean and compactly muscled, its quiet strength obvious in his wrists and his neck and the breadth of his shoulders, but his face was shaded by his hat and, when he glanced up at her from beneath its brim, the lightness of his eyes stopped the breath in Bea's throat.

'Can I ask you something?' he said.

What was he going to ask? If he could take off her hat and run his fingers down her throat? If he could unbutton her shirt? If he could kiss her again, the way he had kissed her in the kitchen? Bea's mind span with the possibilities.

'Yes,' she managed on a gasp. 'Of course.'

'What are you doing here?' he asked, as if he really wanted to know.

Oh.

Bea stared down in her tea, horrified at her own disappointment. 'What do you mean?'

Chase turned back to watch Chloe, his hands clasped loosely around the mug. 'You don't like it here. You don't belong. Why come in the first place?'

'Emily wanted to come,' said Bea, trying not to think about the pang that had gone through her when he had told her that she didn't belong. It was true, but he didn't have to make it sound so…so *definite*. 'Nick told her that you wanted two friends.'

Chase nodded. 'That's right. We've had problems in the past. The cook and the governess end up spending so much time together that if they don't get on, it makes it difficult for everybody.'

'That's what Nick said. Anyway, Emily can't cook—she can barely open a tin of beans—so she asked if I'd come with her.'

'Hasn't she got any other friends she could have asked?'

'None who can cook like I do, and none who owe her like I do,' said Bea wryly.

She saw Chase glance at her in frank disbelief. 'Emily's a bit scatty, I know, but she's been a good friend to me. I always envied her,' she went on after a moment. 'She's so outgoing, and such good fun, and…well, you've seen what she's like. Everybody loves Emily.'

Chase looked sceptical, but he didn't say anything.

'Emily's always got a plan,' Bea tried to explain. 'It's usually romantic and more often than not completely impractical, but at least she knows what she wants, and she isn't afraid to go for it.'

She swirled the tea around in her mug with a sigh. 'I feel such a coward compared to Emily. I don't like change, and I never take risks.' She glanced at Chase. 'You saw what I was like today. Not washing my hair is about as brave as I ever get. Pathetic, isn't it?'

'You came out to Australia,' he pointed out.

'Only because Emily bullied me into it. I'd never have given up my job and my home and my life if it had been up to me. I was quite comfortable as I was. I had a great job doing something I loved, I had a flat I loved, and I was engaged to a man I loved. Why would I want to give up any of that?' she said defensively, as if Chase had accused her of something.

'No reason,' said Chase calmly, but his eyes had narrowed at the mention of Phil.

'I liked my life,' said Bea. 'I didn't want to change anything about it, but it all changed anyway,' she remembered bitterly. The pain was less raw now, but the memories still had the power to hurt her.

Chase wasn't looking at her, and he wasn't probing or exclaiming or demanding to know what had happened. He was just sitting there, listening quietly, and suddenly Bea found herself wanting to tell him anyway.

She took a deep breath. 'Phil and I had been going out for years. We were living together in London, and we'd decided that we'd get married. We had a big engagement party, invited everyone, and started planning the wedding. I was looking at wedding dresses when Phil came home one day and told me that he couldn't go ahead with it.'

'He'd met someone else?'

'My sister.'

A double betrayal. No wonder she was a bit spiky sometimes, thought Chase. 'I'm sorry,' he said after a moment.

'These things happen,' said Bea. She even managed a careless shrug. 'It was probably all for the best, although it didn't feel like it at the time.

'They met at our engagement party. Anna had been away at university, and Phil hadn't seen her for years. Phil said it was like a bolt from the blue for both of them. Now, I think it was brave of him to tell me, and far better then than after we'd married, but at the time I was devastated. I'd had no idea that anything was wrong.'

She shook her head at her own stupidity. She still found it hard to believe that she hadn't been able to read the signs.

'I'd always been the one who had life under control,' she said. 'I was good old Bea, sensible Bea, you can always rely on her, but when I found out about Phil and Anna, I just fell apart. I'd always been close to Anna...' She trailed off, unable to put that particular pain into words.

Chase admired the courageous tilt of her head, the defiant press of her lips. 'What did you do?' he asked quietly.

'Oh, it was all very civilised,' said Bea with a sardonic, sideways look. 'Shouting and screaming wouldn't have changed anything, although Phil and Anna might have felt better if I had. I was just…numb.'

She paused, remembering those terrible days. 'It was Emily who saved me,' she told Chase, getting back to the point. 'She'd been planning to come out to Australia for years. Her mother's Australian, so she doesn't have any visa problems, but she changed all her plans so that I'd be able to come too.

'I didn't have much say in the matter,' said Bea, smiling slightly at the memory of Emily who had come round, or phoned, every day to make sure that she was all right. 'I didn't think I'd like Australia, but Emily insisted. She made all the arrangements, and in the end I was too miserable to care one way or the other. It was Emily who got me on the plane, and out here…and it was the best thing that ever happened to me.

'I fell in love with Australia the moment I stepped off the plane. Coming here changed my life, and I owe that to Emily. That's really why I came out to Calulla Downs,' she told Chase frankly. 'I did it for her.

'And maybe I was hoping that being somewhere I didn't expect to enjoy would make it easier when it came to going home,' she added honestly. 'I've only got another month, and then I have to leave.'

Her mouth turned down at the corners. 'I'm not looking forward to going home. Phil and Anna are getting married soon, and I'm going to have to smile and be nice and pretend I don't mind. It's not going to be easy, is it?'

'I guess that depends whether you *will* be pretending or not,' said Chase. '*Do* you still mind?'

CHAPTER SIX

BEA thought about it, a tiny frown of concentration between her brows. 'I thought I did,' she said slowly, as if it was only just occurring to her. 'I suppose I just got used to the idea of being broken-hearted but…no, I don't think I am any more. I think I mind more about my sister than about Phil, which probably means that it wasn't that great a relationship to start with.

'Emily always said that I was never really in love with Phil,' she went on. 'She thought I was just playing safe, and maybe she was right, but it won't make it any easier to see him with Anna.'

'You know, you'll get used to it,' said Chase, and she turned to him with a sudden surge of bitterness.

'Easy for you to say! You don't know what it was like, discovering that your fiancé is in love with your own sister!'

'Don't I?' he said evenly.

Bea stared at him, and he looked back at her with a crooked smile. 'How do you think Nick met Georgie?' he said.

'*You* were engaged to Georgie Grainger?'

She was so frankly incredulous that Chase couldn't help reflecting that it was just as well he didn't have any false hopes about her opinion of him. He shrugged.

'It wasn't as bad as that. We weren't engaged, but I was in love with her, yes.'

Bea shook her head to clear it. She was still having trouble believing that Chase had ever been involved with anyone as gorgeous and glamorous as Georgie Grainger. 'How…?' she said simply.

'Georgie and I were at school in Brisbane at the same time,' he said, understanding Bea's less than flattering reaction. 'She comes from a station like this one, not so isolated, but still remote enough for the kids all to be sent to boarding school. There were a lot of country kids there. Georgie was a couple of years younger than me, and we used to see each other at school dances, sports, that kind of thing.'

He chucked the dregs of his tea into the dust. 'Georgie wasn't as glossy in those days. She was always really pretty, but she hadn't learned how to dress or how to be a star. She had to be centre of attention, though.'

He grinned affectionately, and Bea was conscious of a sharp pinch of jealousy. 'No one was surprised when she announced that she wanted to be an actress and took herself off to drama school. We'd see each other as often as we could, but it wasn't easy with me out here, and her in Sydney.

'I used to try and get down there every other weekend,' he said, 'and one time I took Nick with me. He's four years older than me, and had been away travelling. We went to see Georgie in some play. I can't remember what it was, only that it was terrible and she was lousy, but Nick couldn't take his eyes off her. We went backstage afterwards and...well, I'm not the most sensitive man on earth, but even I could see what was happening. Three weeks later, Georgie threw in her acting career and married Nick.'

He sounded so matter-of-fact that Bea eyed him curiously. He didn't *seem* broken-hearted, but it was hard to tell what he was thinking sometimes.

'How did you feel?' she asked, and then winced as she realised how fatuous her question must have sounded. She knew better than most people how he must have felt. 'Sorry,' she said inadequately.

'It's OK,' said Chase. 'It was a long time ago. No, it wasn't the best time of my life, but I think I always knew that Georgie was out of my league. I couldn't feel bitter with her, anyway.'

His voice always softened when he talked about Georgie, Bea noticed, and then caught herself up. That wasn't her feeling *jealous,* was it?

'I went off travelling for a couple of years,' he was carrying on, unaware of her mental interruption. 'When I got back, Nick and Georgie were established in the homestead, and I just moved back in with them.'

'Wasn't that awkward?' asked Bea. She couldn't imagine calmly moving in with Phil and Anna.

'It's hard to feel awkward with Georgie, or with Nick, come to that. They can both charm the crocs out of the creek. She's great, Georgie,' said Chase. 'You'd like her.'

Bea wasn't so sure about that.

'You would,' he insisted. 'You think you're not going to, but then you do. Sometimes she drives you wild, of course, but you can never stay cross with her. It's impossible not to like

Georgie,' he assured a still unconvinced Bea. 'She's just…irresistible.'

'You sound like you're still in love with her.'

Uh-oh, that *definitely* sounded like jealousy! And what was worse, Chase obviously thought so, too. He did that business with his eyebrow that never failed to make Bea feel about six inches high.

'Georgie's a very special person,' he said carefully, 'but she isn't easy to live with. I've seen what a dance she leads Nick. Georgie wants everything. She wants Nick, but she wants her career too. She needs applause, and she doesn't get enough to keep her happy in the outback, which is what Nick needs. I'm glad I didn't have to deal with that.'

Obviously he *was* still in love with Georgie, thought Bea, ruffled in a way she couldn't explain. He hadn't denied it anyway, had he?

'So you're not looking for a substitute?' she said, more sharply than she had intended.

'No,' said Chase. 'I'm holding out for a suitable girl.'

Suitable? Hadn't he heard the twentieth century was over, let alone the nineteenth? 'What's a suitable girl?' asked Bea derisively, knowing even as she asked that the answer wasn't going to be anyone like her.

Sure enough, it wasn't.

Chase appeared to take her question seriously. 'A girl who belongs here, who understands the outback,' he said. 'A girl who isn't going to be bored or complain when times are hard. A girl who's prepared to work as hard as I am.'

'You're asking a lot,' said Bea. 'Don't you think that's a bit demanding?'

'I think it's realistic,' said Chase flatly. 'Calulla Downs is home, but I want my own place eventually. I've heard rumours that a property on the other side of Mackinnon is coming up for sale. It's been run down for years, so it would mean starting again, and it wouldn't be easy. Someone who spent her time hankering after shops or movies or smart restaurants would be no use to me.'

Someone like you. He might as well have come right out and said it, thought Bea peevishly. She was the opposite of what he wanted.

Which was just as well, she pointed out to herself as she lay in bed that night. The isolation of Calulla Downs must be going to her head. She had an uncomfortably distinct memory of sitting by the waterhole and wanting him to kiss her, and really, what would have been the point of that?

What would be the point of getting over Phil only to fall for someone who not only had nothing in common with her but was obviously still in love with someone else? And not just any old someone else, but a beautiful, glamorous, talented, charming actress. Your rival from hell, in fact.

So, no, she absolutely, definitely was not going to do anything stupid like that. *I've got no intention of sleeping with you, falling in love with you or wanting to marry you,* she had told Chase, and she meant it. A relationship involving any of the three would be doomed to disaster from the start, and Bea had been hurt enough.

Baz was leaving on Monday, so Bea wasn't surprised when Emily didn't turn up that night. She presumed that they were saying their goodbyes, and hoped that Emily wasn't going to get too tearful.

But when Emily appeared the next morning after Chase and the remaining stockmen had left, she was all smiles.

'I've come to say goodbye,' she said hugging Bea.

Bea pulled back and looked at her friend with foreboding. 'Goodbye?'

'I'm leaving with Baz. He's taking me home to meet his parents!' Emily twirled Bea ecstatically around the room. 'I'm so happy!' she cried. 'I knew that coming here would change my life. It's as if it was *meant* to be! Oh, thank you, thank you, thank you, darling Bea, for agreeing to come! If you hadn't, I'd never have met Baz, and think how terrible that would have been!'

'But, Emily, what are you going to do?'

Emily flung her arms wide. 'I'm just going to be with Baz. What more do I need?'

'What about your job here?'

'Baz is more important,' Emily declared. 'I thought you'd be pleased, Bea,' she went on, hurt by Bea's lack of enthusiasm. 'It means that you can go back to Sydney straight away. You never wanted to be here in the first place.'

'Who would do the cooking? And what about Chloe? I can hardly walk out and leave her to look after herself,' Bea pointed out, having checked that Chloe was out of earshot.

'That grumpy old Chase can get someone new,' said Emily airily. 'Baz says he turns over girls every month or so, so he's bound to be able to replace you really easily.'

Somehow, this wasn't what Bea wanted to hear.

Emily's mind had already flitted back to Baz. Beaming, she sat on the table and swung her legs. 'Oh, Bea, I'm so happy I can't tell you! I wish you could be in love like this, too.'

'I'm not sure I want to be if it means losing my mind,' said Bea crisply. 'I can't believe you're seriously talking about taking off with Baz. You hardly know anything about him!'

'I know I'm in love, and that's all that matters.' Emily jumped off the table, too excited to keep still. 'Now, don't fuss, Bea. Go back to Sydney and I'll contact you there when I know where we're going to be. If you're still around, I'll invite you to my wedding.'

Bea goggled at her. 'Baz has asked you to *marry* him?'

'Well, not in so many words,' Emily admitted, which was no surprise to Bea. Baz wasn't big on words. 'We don't need things cut and dried like you do. We just know each other instinctively, and I just *know* this is right and Baz is The One.'

There was no point in trying to argue with Emily when she was in this kind of mood, as Bea knew to her cost. She sighed, foreseeing just how well this was going to go down with Chase.

'When are you planning to leave?'

'This morning. Baz is just putting his things in the ute, and we'll go as soon as I've packed my stuff.'

'I don't think Chase will be back until lunchtime,' said Bea, but even as she opened her mouth she knew what Emily was going to say.

'You'll explain how it is for me, won't you, Bea?' she pleaded. 'I find him a bit intimidating, and I know if I try to explain about Baz and falling in love, he just won't understand.'

Chase wasn't quite such a stranger to love as Emily seemed to imagine, but Bea didn't think there was much point in explaining that. He was still unlikely to be very sympathetic when he found that Emily was leaving.

'It's not as if Chase cares whether we're here or not, as long as there's someone to cook the meals and keep an eye on Chloe,' Emily was saying.

She was probably right, Bea thought, depressed, as Emily flitted off to throw her clothes in her suitcase.

A few minutes later, Baz tooted his car horn at the bottom of the veranda steps. Emily gave him her suitcase to throw in the back, hugged Chloe and Bea, climbed in beside Baz and drove off with a cheerful wave.

Chase was furious, just as Bea had known he would be. She had to break the news when he came back at lunchtime, and she hadn't enjoyed the experience. She had never seen him lose his temper before.

'I suppose you're going to want to go now, too?' he said in a savage voice as he paced angrily around the kitchen.

'I won't go until you've found someone to replace us,' said Bea, quailing but trying not to show it.

'Too right you won't!' Chase glowered at her as if Emily's irresponsibility was all her fault. 'You can look after Chloe as well, and if Emily thinks I'm going to forward her wages, she can think again.'

'I'm sure she won't,' Bea tried unsuccessfully to placate him. 'She may be a bit thoughtless, but she's doesn't care about money at all.'

'Just as well, if she's thrown her lot in with Baz,' he said with a snort. 'She's a fool if she thinks that relationship will last the month!'

Bea had her own doubts on that score, but she thought it would be better to keep her mouth shut for now. Saying anything would only antagonise him even more, and he looked thunderous enough as it was. His brows were drawn together in a ferocious line and a muscle jumped angrily in his tense jaw, which made it all the harder to understand why she should have this inexplicable longing to put her arms around him and assure him that everything would work out fine and kiss the last of his fury away.

Unsurprisingly, Chase showed no sign that he would appreciate such a gesture, even if she had given in to such a bizarre urge. He was striding around the kitchen, oblivious to Chloe's wide-eyed stare, ranting and raving about Emily.

'I'm sick of you girls coming out here and playing at being in the outback. You think you can turn up, enjoy our quaint little ways for a while and then swan off again as soon as you get bored or are panting after some man. You don't seem to understand that this isn't a game for us. We've got work to do. I've got ten thousand head of cattle out there to get through the yards, but I don't suppose Emily gave that a thought!'

The chances of Emily knowing or caring about Chase's cattle were zilch, Bea thought privately, but it didn't seem tactful to say so.

'It's bad enough losing an experienced stockman like Baz without having to run around after governesses and cooks,' Chase was storming. 'I haven't got time to find a replacement right now, so I don't care how much you're pining to get back to your precious city, you can just stay here and do the job you're being paid to do until I have!'

And with that, he slammed out. The screen door clattered alarmingly in his wake, and the wooden steps from the veranda reverberated with the angry strike of his boots.

Bea didn't blame him, but when she turned back to Chloe, she saw that the little girl was looking upset. She wasn't used to seeing her uncle lose his temper like that.

'Uncle Chase is cross,' she said, and her little mouth wobbled.

Bea took her on her lap and gave her a cuddle. 'Don't worry about it, Chloe,' she said. 'He's not cross with you.'

'Is he cross with you?'

'A bit.'

'Why?'

She should have known *that* was coming. 'Because he's cross with Emily, but she's not here, so I'm the next best thing. He has to be cross with somebody, otherwise he might burst!'

Chloe giggled, her wobble forgotten. 'Would he go pop?'

'He would. And we don't want that, do we?'

Bea wished she could be reassured as easily as Chloe. She might understand Chase's anger, but that didn't mean that she had liked being on the receiving end of it.

The implication that she was like all the other girls who came out here had hurt. She wasn't playing at being in the outback, she didn't find him or his way of life the slightest bit quaint, and *she* hadn't left him in the lurch! Chase only had his cows to deal with; now she had two jobs to do.

It was a long afternoon. Bea hadn't appreciated before just what a difference Emily had made. It wasn't so much that Chloe was difficult but, without Emily, Bea had to be constantly aware of where she was and what she was doing. If Chloe wasn't there, she had to keep checking on her to make sure she was all right, and if she was, she talked constantly, which made it extremely difficult for Bea to concentrate on what she was doing. The meal that night was not going to be up to her usual standard, she thought, resigned.

When Chase came back, Bea and Chloe were on the veranda. Chloe had insisted on having her hair washed, and Bea was combing out the tangles. She was sitting on the wooden bench where they had smoko every morning, Chloe pinned between her knees, and ignoring her vociferous complaints. 'If you stand still, I won't need to pull,' she said.

Chase watched them from across the yard. It had seemed a very long afternoon to him, too. He knew that he had overreacted to Emily's departure, and he had a nasty feeling that part of the reason for his fury was the thought that Bea would take the opportunity to leave too.

And part was anger with himself for caring whether she did or not.

The thing was, he'd got used to Bea being there. Chase had spent the afternoon trying to convince himself that it would better if she went sooner rather than later. There was no point in getting used to her. She had made no secret of the fact that she was a city girl, through and through. She didn't like the outback. She was uptight and prickly and she wasted a ridiculous amount of time on her appearance every day. She was the last person who would ever belong out here.

So why did his stride increase as he got closer to the homestead? Why did his heart feel lighter when he went into the kitchen and saw her standing at the cooker, stirring gravy, her face pink from the heat, or moving around the long table, setting out knives and forks, that hair that was such a bother to her tucked behind her ear?

Why did he hate the thought of sitting out on the veranda in the dark without her?

Chloe saw him first. 'Uncle Chase!' Wriggling out of Bea's grasp, she ran down the steps towards him and let him swing her into the air. 'Bea was pulling my hair,' she complained.

'Don't tell tales,' said Chase, carrying her back up the steps. 'And anyway, it didn't look like she was pulling it to me.' He put Chloe down and pushed her gently back towards Bea. 'You let her finish combing your hair.'

After that first heart-stopping moment when she caught sight of him, Bea was doing her best to appear normal. She went back to untangling Chloe's hair with unnatural concentration.

'You were very cross before,' Chloe told her uncle.

'I know,' he said.

'Bea says you had to shout at her or you would have gone pop!' She stuck out her tummy and mimed it bursting with so much of her mother's dramatic flair that Chase laughed, albeit ruefully.

'As usual, Bea was quite right,' he said.

He sat down on the bench next to Bea and placed his hat between them. 'I'm sorry about earlier,' he said.

'It doesn't matter,' said Bea, who had fully intended to remain aloof. 'You were entitled to be angry.'

'I shouldn't have taken it out on you, though.' He cleared his throat. 'I know you'll want to get back to Sydney as soon as you can, but would you mind staying until I can find someone else?' It was what he should have asked her before, instead of ordering her to stay.

'I said I'd stay a month, and I will,' said Bea, not meeting his eyes. She gave Chloe's hair a last comb and let her go. 'I'm used to things now, and I'm fond of Chloe,' she added hastily in case he started getting the wrong idea. 'It's only for another couple of weeks in any case. I don't mind staying as we agreed until Nick comes home.'

Chase was taken aback at how relieved he felt. He studied her profile, reluctant to exploit her guilt about Emily. 'I thought you were desperate to get back to Sydney,' he said.

'I am, but I'm running out of time on my visa. It's not worth me getting another job, so I may as well stay here where it's cheap.

There's nothing to spend my money on, so I could use my wages to spend my last two or three weeks travelling.'

Put like that, it sounded quite convincing, Bea congratulated herself. It sounded as if she was staying for purely practical reasons, and not because she particularly wanted to.

'Are you sure you're not saying that because you feel responsible for Emily?' Chase asked suspiciously. 'There's no need for you to stay that long if you don't want to. I could probably arrange to get someone here by the end of the week.'

What did he want her to do? Beg him to let her stay? 'Look, if you'd rather get someone more suitable, just say so,' snapped Bea. '*I* don't mind,' she lied.

'No, no,' said Chase hurriedly. 'I want you to stay, if you really don't mind.' He paused and looked at Bea, whose head was tilted at a characteristic angle. Her cheeks were flushed and her eyes were bright with an edgy sort of defiance.

She would be here for another fortnight. Another two weeks of not having to think about who was going to cook the meals or worry about who was looking after Chloe. Two weeks of not having to deal with Georgie's guests.

Two weeks of coming home and finding her here at the end of the day.

How did he thank Bea for that? A simple thank you would sound hopelessly inadequate, but in the end it was all Chase could think of, so he said it anyway.

'Thank you,' he said.

I'm not having anything to do with children. Wasn't that what she had insisted to Emily? Look at her now, thought Bea as she tucked Chloe up in bed that night. She was turning into a regular Julie Andrews. She would be bursting into song next.

'Sleep tight,' she said as Chloe wrapped her arms round her neck in one of her throttling hugs.

Watching from the door, Chase was aware of something alarmingly like jealousy. He wished that he could pull Bea down to him the way Chloe could, and feel her hair swinging softly against his skin. When he bent to kiss Chloe's cheek in his turn, he could smell the lingering traces of Bea's perfume.

'Bea smells nice,' said Chloe, reading his thoughts with uncanny accuracy.

'I know,' said Chase.

He found Bea moving briskly around the kitchen. 'Thanks for looking after Chloe today,' he said.

'That's OK,' she said, carefully casual as she turned the potatoes. 'It's a new experience for me, being with children. I've never had anything to do with them before.'

'I wouldn't have guessed. Chloe likes you.'

'Chloe likes everybody,' said Bea, forgetting how wary Chloe had been when they first arrived.

'I don't know about that,' said Chase. 'She's made life very difficult for some of the girls who've been here.'

Had Chloe been difficult for Kirsty and Sue and all those other girlfriends whose names Chase had struggled to remember? Bea was ashamed of herself for hoping so.

'It can't be easy for her with people coming and going all the time,' she commented instead. 'She must miss her mother.'

'You've got to remember that Chloe's never had her mother there the whole time,' said Chase. 'It's not that Georgie doesn't love her— she does—but they decided that it would be better for Chloe to stay here with Nick rather than be dragged around hotel rooms and film sets.'

He looked at Bea with a kind of baffled frustration as she stood at the cooker with her back to him. Why were they talking about Nick and Georgie's childcare arrangements? he wondered wildly, when all he wanted to do was go over and kiss the back of her neck, to put his arms around her and tell her how glad he was that she was staying.

But Bea was busy lifting lids on saucepans and stirring things, and there was tension in her spine. She wasn't taking any notice of him, probably wasn't even looking at him, Chase realised. She wouldn't lean back against him with a shudder of pleasure, or turn in his arms and smile.

She was much more likely to be horrified, and he wouldn't be able to blame her. Bea was doing him a favour by agreeing to stay on for a while. After the way he'd shouted at her earlier, he was lucky she hadn't walked out there and then. As it was, if he made a move now, she'd just think that he was taking advantage of the fact that they would be alone together in the homestead tonight, without even Emily's nominal presence.

She might even be nervous about the possibility, Chase thought, appalled. It would explain why she held herself so tensely, her body language practically screaming, Keep your hands to yourself!

So he kept his hands to himself and, muttering something about a shower, he left Bea to her cooking.

They had coffee as usual on the veranda after the stockmen had left that night. Bea thought about going straight to bed, but that would look as if she was nervous about being alone with Chase, which she definitely *wasn't*.

She was just wondering why she hadn't accepted his offer to find another cook by the end of the week and gone while she had the chance. Now she had let herself in for another fortnight of sitting edgily next to him and trying not to think about that time he had kissed her.

She hadn't even managed to maintain a cool distance after being shouted at like that. She should have held out for a grovelling apology, but oh, no! all Chase had had to do was sit down next to her. It was pathetic, thought Bea, despising herself. Anyone would think that she *wanted* to stay!

The silence stretched awkwardly between them. Bea was acutely conscious of Chase beside her, very still and self-contained and somehow definite in the dim light. Beyond the veranda, it was very dark. The blue light in the yard went *psst, psst, psst* with each doomed insect. The faint crackling noise made Bea think of the way her nerves jumped whenever Chase lifted his mug, or leant forward to rest his arms on his knees and look out into the night.

The stiller he sat, the more Bea fidgeted. The silence might not bother him, but it was making her twitchy.

'It's quiet without Emily,' she tried at last.

'Yes.'

'Not that she was ever here at this time.'

'No.'

It was like trying to make conversation with one of the cattle dogs that lay panting in the shade all day. Worse, in fact. At least the dogs wagged their tails and looked pleased when she stopped to give them a word.

Sipping her coffee, Bea racked her brains for something else she could say that wouldn't make him think that she was even aware of the fact that he was a man and she was a woman and that to all intents and purposes they were quite alone in the dark.

'Look,' said Chase suddenly, making her arm jerk and spilling coffee down her front.

He stopped.

'What?' said Bea as she brushed ineffectively at the drops.

'You seem a bit tense,' he commented.

'I'm not the slightest bit tense!' she said tensely.

'OK, great,' said Chase. 'But if you *were,* I just thought I should say that you don't need to worry about…well, the two of us being alone together.'

Bea managed an unsuccessful laugh. 'We're hardly alone. There's Chloe, four stockmen, the married man and his wife…it's a positive crowd.'

At least Chase didn't point out, as he could have done, that most of the 'crowd' was well out of earshot.

'If you're not worried, that's fine,' he said.

'Of course I'm not worried,' snapped Bea, and then spoilt it by adding childishly, 'I know how you despise us English girls!'

Chase turned to stare at her. 'I don't despise you. I'm very grateful to you.'

Grateful? What self-respecting girl wanted a man to be *grateful?*

His reasonable tone only made Bea feel even more childish. 'Good,' she retorted. 'So I'm not worried about you, and you *certainly* don't need to worry about being alone with me!'

Chase had known that all along.

It was a relief to both of them that more guests were booked to arrive the next day. Chase flew to collect them from the airport in Mackinnon, and Bea threw herself into preparations for their arrival and tried to forget the restless night she had spent, wondering what it would have been like if Chase hadn't made it crystal clear that he had no intention of laying a finger on her.

Wondering what it would have been like if he had given her reason to be worried, if he *had* suggested that they could make the most of the fact that they were alone in the quiet outback night. What had kept Bea awake most of the night was the fear that the only thing that would have really worried her would have been her own ability to resist.

Which was stupid. She had already decided, very sensibly, that there was no point in getting involved with a man like Chase. This wasn't the time or place to get tired of being sensible.

The guests were boisterous and good-humoured and determined to enjoy every minute of their stay. They liked to help in the kitchen and to sit out on the veranda at night, which meant that there was no opportunity to be alone with Chase any more.

Bea told herself that she was glad. She was busy enough, what with cooking and cleaning and Chloe, and running around after five guests. That was what she was here for, she reminded herself sternly. She wasn't here to listen out for the sound of Chase's step outside, to wait for him to come and join them at table, or to look out for his rare, illuminating smile.

She knew that he regarded looking after the guests as a chore he had been landed with in Nick and Georgie's absence, but the guests themselves would never have guessed that he was anything less than an eager host. He could be charming when he wanted to, Bea observed somewhat jealously. He was never like that with her. She might as well not have existed for all the attention he paid her now.

Not that she cared, of course.

CHAPTER SEVEN

ON THE third day of the visit, Chase had succumbed and agreed to let the guests take part
in the muster. Bea got up even earlier than
usual to send them all off with a big breakfast
and, while the stockmen were saddling up the
horses, Chase gave Bea instructions as to how
to reach the stopping place. 'Can you bring
lunch out to us? We should be there just after
midday.'

He drew her a map on the kitchen table, but
Bea was distracted by his deft brown fingers
moving over the paper in swift, sure movements, marking out paddocks and creeks and
dams. He was leaning on the table next to her
chair, his arm very close to hers, his shirt care-
lessly rolled up. She could see the fine, flat
hairs at his strong wrist and the frayed strap of
his watch.

Bea could feel herself being drawn irresisti-
bly into the hard body so close to hers, a ter-
rifying feeling, and the image of giving and
simply suckering against him was so vivid that

she had to lean right over the other way in compensation. Chase cast her a curious look.

'Have you got that?'

'Um…yes,…over the third cattle grid…'

Chase sighed and straightened. 'Don't forget to bring this with you,' he said, pushing the paper towards her. 'If things get really bad, Chloe can probably show you the way.'

It was a huge relief when he moved away.

Outside, the horses were ready, shaking their heads up and down and jingling their harness, as the guests milled excitedly around. Bea took out some flapjacks for them to have at smoko, and they commiserated with her for being left behind.

'I don't mind,' said Bea, not entirely truthfully. 'Musters aren't really my thing.'

They weren't, of course, but it didn't stop her feeling left out when she eventually found them all sitting round a fire with Chase and the stockmen, waiting for the billies to boil. The horses were tethered nearby, and wherever Bea looked there were cattle browsing, grateful for a pause in being herded headlong through the bush.

'Here they are!' cried Janet, and waved as Bea drew up and parked Chase's big four-wheel-drive in the shade.

Chase turned to see Bea jump down from the driver's seat and reach back inside for a basket of sandwiches. She looked gloriously out of place as usual in tailored shorts and a pale pink shirt, with pearls, for God's sake. He was surprised she wasn't wearing high heels.

Her hair was dried into a neat, conker-brown bob that swung as she walked towards them, Chloe running ahead. When she got closer, Chase could see that she had her aloof expression on, the one which meant that she was more unsure of herself than she wanted to admit.

He got up to take the basket from her. 'I see you found us.'

'Eventually,' said Bea a little tightly, and Chloe tugged at his arm.

'Bea got lost. She said your map was stupid!'

They all laughed, although Bea's smile was decidedly frayed at the edges. She had been driving around for what seemed like hours across flat, brown paddocks that all looked exactly the same as the last one. In the alien landscape, she found herself getting hot and panicky, and she had turned the map round and round on the steering wheel, trying to make sense of it.

In the end it had been Chloe who had pointed her in the right direction. She was the one who was stupid, not the map, and getting here to find Chase looking lean and easy and utterly at home hadn't made her feel any better.

Forcing a smile, she sat on a worn log next to Janet and tried not to watch Chase as he passed the sandwiches around. Janet was full of the morning they had had. Bea only listened with half an ear until Janet heaved an envious sigh. 'You're so lucky to have a guy like Chase,' she said.

Bea sat abruptly upright. 'Sorry?'

'You and Chase…May and I were just saying this morning how lucky we think you are.'

'That's right.' May joined in the conversation, leaning across Chase and beaming at Bea. 'We were wishing we were twenty years younger!'

Appalled at the misunderstanding, Bea stared from one to the other. 'Oh, but we're not—' She broke off, not sure how to put it.

'You're *not?*' Janet looked back at her, evidently unable to decide whether Bea was joking or not.

'No! I mean, I just work here.'

'You don't mean it?' Janet shook her head in amazement. 'Hey, did you hear that?' she said to the others sitting round the fire. 'Bea and Chase aren't a couple! We were so sure, too, weren't we, May?'

May nodded vigorously. 'We've noticed the way you look at each other.'

Bea was poppy red by now, not even daring to look at Chase. 'No, there's nothing like that.'

'Well, why not?' May's husband, Ron, a big, jovial man, dug Chase in the ribs with his elbow. 'A great little cook like Bea! I'd snap her up if I were you!'

Chase's eyes flickered to Bea, who was sitting bolt upright on her log, scarlet-cheeked and clearly wishing that she was anywhere other than here. He managed a thin smile. 'I think Bea has other plans,' he said.

'Oh, come on! What girl's going to turn down the chance of a fine man like you? You make sure of her while you've got the chance. You'll be sorry if you let her go.'

It went on like that for the next two days. For some reason, May and Ron and their friends had decided that Bea and Chase were meant for each other, and if they weren't already carrying on secretly then they ought to be. They thought it was a great joke, and missed no chance to tease Bea with sly references to their supposed passionate affair or to josh Chase about what a lucky man he was, while Bea and Chase's smiles grew more and more fixed.

Having welcomed their arrival as a distraction, Bea now couldn't wait for them to go. She waved them off at last, feeling sorry for Chase who was doomed to another couple of hours of winks and nods and pointed comments as he flew them back to Mackinnon.

At least the atmosphere between the two of them had improved, she thought, walking back into the homestead. Not that they'd spent any time together. If they'd so much as bumped into each other on the veranda, Ron and the others would have pounced on it as evidence of an assignation! But she'd caught Chase's eye once or twice, enough to know that they were united in the gritting of their teeth if nothing else.

'Thank God they've gone,' she sighed that night as she threw herself down next to Chase and savoured the silence.

'I know. No more demands to be invited to the wedding!'

'No more laboured jokes, or heavy hints about what a great couple we would be!'

'No more wondering aloud what we got up to the moment we left the room.'

'Or why we were pretending to sleep in separate rooms.'

Chase smiled as he shook his head. 'They were terrible, weren't they?'

'Honestly, you'd think there was something wrong with us for not tearing our clothes off at every opportunity,' complained Bea. 'I think they were amazed that we could keep our hands off each other!'

There was a sudden pause.

Bea could have bitten her tongue out. See how easily it happened! A few careless words, and without warning the shared laughter had turned into something else, something deep and disturbing, something that tightened the air between them and made her heart slam in slow, painful strokes against her ribs.

'Just out of interest,' said Chase conversationally, 'why aren't we tearing each other's clothes off?'

'Because…we're not interested in each other that way,' said Bea with difficulty.

'Oh. Right.'

'And because you're not my type.'

He turned to face her. 'I see.'

'And I'm not yours.'

This time Chase didn't say anything. He just looked at her mouth.

'And…and because I'm leaving next week.'

Silence. Bea's heart was booming and thudding and breathing was strangely difficult.

He was going to kiss her. Oh, please, please let him kiss her.

'Look at me, Bea,' said Chase softly at last, and it took every ounce of Bea's will not to turn her head.

She was thinking about all the other girls who had sat here in the dark with him. *Look at me, Kirsty,* he had probably said then, too. *Look at me, Sue. Look at me, Sara.* She didn't want to join the end of that particular line.

Or did she?

Bea was uncomfortably aware that it might be *exactly* what she wanted right then. For some reason an old cliché was running round her head, 'a taste of honey is better than none at all'. Or should that have been 'worse than none at all'?

Bea was still trying to remember when all her senses snarled as Chase reached out and smoothed a strand of hair behind her ear, very gently.

'Remember your challenge?' he asked.

She swallowed, distracted by the burning of her skin where his fingers had grazed her cheek. 'Wh-what challenge?'

'You said that you weren't going to sleep with me,' Chase reminded her. 'You weren't going to fall in love with me and you weren't going to marry me.'

'Oh, yes.' Bea remembered now. She couldn't help wishing she hadn't been quite so dogmatic about it. She moistened her lips. 'Well, not much has changed. I'm certainly not going to marry you,' she said bravely.

'No, that wouldn't be a good idea at all,' he agreed. 'You'd be a very unsuitable wife for me.' But there was a thread of laughter in his voice and his hand was drifting tantalisingly in her hair.

She forced her mind back with an effort. 'And I'm not going to fall in love with you,' she said.

Not very much, anyway. Deep down, Bea had a nasty feeling that she *might* be a little bit in love with him already. Only a very little bit, though. The bit that would be satisfied if he would just take her to bed and make long, sweet love to her right now.

But that wasn't the same as being really in love with him, was it?

'I'm not going to fall in love with you, either,' Chase said, moving closer along the bench and telling himself that he believed it.

'So that just leaves sleeping together, doesn't it?'

'Yes,' she said, ridiculously breathless. She couldn't manage anything else.

If she was sensible, she would get up and go right now. The trouble was that she didn't want to be sensible, not here, not now, not with Chase so close beside her, smiling in a way that made her skin shiver with anticipation.

'Do you think you might be up for negotiation on that one?' he murmured, and Bea couldn't stop an answering smile tugging at her mouth.

'I might be.'

'We-el,' he said slowly, pretending to consider, 'since you're not going to fall in love, I wondered how you felt about a meaningless, short-term relationship?'

That ought to reassure her that they didn't need to take this too seriously, Chase told himself. If he was honest, a meaningful, long-term relationship didn't sound too bad right then, but Bea might back off if she felt that he was too keen. Being involved was too close to being in love, and neither of them wanted that.

And, in the meantime, a meaningless, short-term relationship with her was better than nothing.

A lot better.

'Would it involve some tearing off of clothes and not being able to keep our hands off each other?' she said a little shakily.

'Oh, yes,' Chase promised, his hand tightening at the nape of her neck to pull her towards him. 'There'd be lots of that...just to please our late guests, of course!'

'In that case,' Bea smiled against his mouth as she succumbed to temptation, 'I think I might change my mind about the first part of my challenge.'

And then she stopped smiling as his lips claimed hers, and she was lost beneath a warm, rolling tide of sheer, wicked pleasure that went on and on as he pulled her onto his lap and they kissed and kissed and kissed again, the way Bea had been trying not to think about kissing him all this time.

How could she have resisted something that felt so good? she wondered, but it was her last coherent thought for a very long time.

'I think it's time we tore off some of those clothes, don't you?' said Chase unevenly at last.

It took them a while as they kept stopping to kiss on the way, but at length he was able to pull her into his room and swing her back into his arms, pressing her back against the door. They kissed with increasing urgency until Bea was gasping and giddy with excitement. She fumbled with the buttons of his shirt, tugging it from his trousers so that she could slide her arms around his bare back and kiss his throat, while Chase's hands moved insistently over her.

He was trying to find a way to unfasten her dress, and finally located the zip under her arm.

'Ah!' he murmured with satisfaction, kissing his way along her shoulder, and slid the zip down after a brief, frustrating struggle to undo the hook at the top. But at last he was able to push the dress down over her hips until it fell into a puddle of material at Bea's feet.

Then they were moving across the room, kissing and shedding the last of their clothes as they went, falling together onto the bed. Bea was lost, and she didn't care. There was only the feel of his body and the taste of his skin, only his strong, sure hands unlocking her, his mouth making her arch against him. The differences between them were forgotten in the pounding excitement as they moved together in a timeless, throbbing, relentless rhythm that ended only when Bea felt her senses explode in a joyful release.

Afterwards, they lay breathless, Bea's body still twitching and tingling with pleasure. 'I think we just made May and Ron very happy,' she said when she was able to speak.

'Who cares about them?' said Chase lazily into her throat. 'We just made *me* very happy.'

Careful, thought Bea as her heart turned over. This was just a short-term romance. It wouldn't do to forget that. But still she couldn't stop her hands smoothing over his back, loving the feel of his firm, sleek body and the way his muscles flexed in response to her touch.

She stretched luxuriously beneath him. 'I've been thinking about this for quite a while,' she confessed, and Chase raised himself up on one elbow to look down into her face with a slow smile.

'So have I. Since the day I walked into the airport at Mackinnon and saw you standing there with your high heels, and your nose in the air.'

'I don't believe you!'

'Well, maybe not right then,' he conceded, smoothing the hair from her face, 'but it wasn't long after that. Definitely since that day at the waterhole.'

'I wish you'd said something sooner.'

Chase rolled onto his back. 'You said you weren't interested,' he reminded her.

Oh, well, if he was going to be put off *that* easily…!

'I didn't want to be just another cook to join the queue.' Bea told the truth, and he turned his head on the pillow. In the starlight, she could see that his expression was serious.

'You would never be that, Bea.'

'It's all right.' Bea was suddenly afraid that she might have given too much of herself away. It would be awfully easy for Chase to misinterpret the way she had cried out his name, for instance. The way her hands had moved hungrily over him. The way she had kissed him just as if she had been in love with him.

It wouldn't do for Chase to think that. It would spoil everything.

'I don't want you to tell me I'm different,' she insisted. 'I'm leaving soon, and this is just a physical thing, right?' If she said it often enough, she might even believe it.

'Right,' said Chase after a tiny pause.

'This is me living dangerously at last!'

'Not that dangerously. We were careful.'

'I don't mean that. I mean doing something without thinking about the consequences and what might happen in the future, and you know what?' said Bea, shifting over so that she could spread her hand over his hard stomach. 'It feels good. In fact, it feels more than good. It feels fantastic!'

Chase pulled her back against him as her fingers drifted tantalisingly. He wouldn't think about the future now. For now she was here in his arms, and that was enough. 'It certainly does!' he murmured.

Bea floated through the next few days, adrift in a tingling, satisfied glow. She wouldn't let herself think about the future. She couldn't think about anything but the night to come, and Chase with his hard hands and his hard body and his cool, firm mouth. All she had to do was look at him and her bones dissolved with desire. It was hard to believe now that she had once disliked him or dismissed him as ordinary.

'Why don't you dry your hair any more?' Chloe demanded one morning.

'I haven't really got time now that Emily's gone,' said Bea, but she didn't meet Chloe's eyes. The truth was that Chase loved to tangle his fingers in her wild curls and so she left it for him.

Chloe was still suspicious of Bea's uncharacteristic behaviour. 'You're always humming now,' she said accusingly.

'That's because I'm happy.'

It was true. There was a lot to be said for a short-term meaningless relationship, Bea told herself. No complications, no anguished wondering about how Chase really felt. They weren't asking anything of each other which meant they could just enjoy the way their differences dissolved in the heart-stopping excitement of the long, sweet nights they shared.

If, once or twice, Bea's thoughts touched on what would happen when her time at Calulla Downs came to an end, they veered quickly away before she had a chance to imagine it, and she closed her mind firmly to the prospect of saying goodbye.

Chase never mentioned it either. Why should he? It wasn't as if they were in love, Bea reminded herself. Their relationship was a purely physical one, they both knew that, and for now that was enough.

And things just kept getting better. Bea was in thrall to the touch of Chase's hands, of his mouth, to the feel of his body. He made her feel beautiful and sexy and exciting in a way Phil had never been able to do. Every evening she would sit across the table from Chase, her body thumping with the promise of the night to come, and she would will the poor stockmen to finish their pudding and leave.

By the middle of the next week, Bea had lost all track of time as the days and nights drifted lazily into each other. When she met Chase's eyes, over supper that night, she wondered how she could ever have thought of them as cold. Had there really been a time when she had been nervous about being alone with him, and the stockmen had seemed to bolt their food and disappear all too soon?

Now the meal seemed endless. It was gratifying that they appeared to enjoy her cooking so much, but Bea longed for them to go. At last it was over, and she leapt to her feet to clear away while Chase had a word with the men outside.

She was already washing the pots at the sink when she heard the screen door creak behind her. She didn't turn round. She knew that Chase was watching her, knew that he wanted her, and she smiled down into the soapy water.

When he came over to brush her hair aside and press his lips to the nape of her neck, she went weak at the knees but somehow managed to carry on washing up.

'Leave it,' he murmured, untying her apron.

'I can't,' said Bea unevenly. 'It's a matter of principle with me to always leave the kitchen clear for the morning.'

'We can wash up later,' said Chase. His lips drifted down her throat as he turned her to face him, unwinding her resistance as she went.

Bea held up her hands in her rubber gloves to stop them dripping on him while he pulled the apron over her head and discarded it. 'I can't leave the kitchen until it's done,' she said provocatively, just to prolong his delicious assault on her senses. They both knew that she was going to succumb in the end.

'We don't need to leave.' Chase smiled as he kissed his way back up her throat to her mouth. 'We can do it right here.'

Breathless, Bea let him tug the rubber gloves from her hands. 'On the kitchen table?'

'Why not?'

With a grunt of satisfaction, he peeled the second glove off and dropped it to the floor so that he could pull her against him. Bea wound her arms around his neck and sank into his kiss.

'It doesn't look very comfortable,' she murmured.

Chase's hand was already sliding up her thigh. 'You won't know until you try it,' he said, and Bea was just about to give in, unable to put up more than a token struggle, when the phone in the office down the corridor started to ring, and they both froze.

They had so few calls that the sound of the phone was startling at the best of times, and now it rang insistently, jarringly, in the silence, impossible to ignore.

Chase cursed under his breath. 'That'll be Nick. No one else would call at this time.'

'You'd better go,' said Bea reluctantly. 'It might be important.'

He kissed her hard, once, and released her. 'Don't put those gloves on again,' he said. 'I'll be back as soon as I've got rid of Nick.'

In fact, Bea had had time to finish the washing up and wipe down the surfaces before Chase reappeared. He had been on the phone for so long that she was afraid that it might be bad news, and it was a huge relief to see that his expression was odd rather than grief-stricken.

'Sorry I was so long. I had Nick and Georgie on the line, and I couldn't shut either of them up.'

'Has something happened?'

'They're back together again,' said Chase. 'They've sorted everything out, are blissfully happy and Georgie tells me that they're going to live happily ever after.'

'That's good news, isn't it?' said Bea doubtfully, confused by his tone, while a cold voice inside her wondered whether it hurt him to hear that his brother was happy again with the woman he had once loved.

'Oh, yes, it's good news. Good for them, anyway.'

Chase raked his fingers through his hair. He felt irritated and unsettled, and more than a little frustrated at having been dragged away from Bea to listen to Nick raving on and on about Georgie. He was glad that they were both so happy, of course, but it had brought home to him that his own relationship with Bea was all too temporary. There would be no living happily ever after for them. Bea would go back to her city and he...he would miss her.

But he couldn't tell her that. Meaningless, short-term, no commitments and no demands...that was the way they had agreed it would be.

'They're so happy, in fact, that they can't bear to be separated again,' he went on. 'They've decided Nick will stay over there until Georgie has finished filming, and then they'll come home together.'

'When will that be?' asked Bea, pulling off her gloves on her own this time.

'A couple of months. They're going to make it a second honeymoon.'

'Two *months?*' She stared at him in dismay. 'What about Chloe?'

'They wanted to know how she was, and I said that she seemed perfectly happy, so Georgie asked if I would carry on as things are rather than uprooting her at this stage.'

Georgie again, Bea noted jealously. 'What did you say?'

'What could I say? I can hardly put Chloe on a plane to LA and ask her to find her parents herself.' Chase looked at Bea. 'I suppose you wouldn't consider staying on a bit longer, would you?' he asked, carefully casual.

'I can't, Chase.' The full realisation of how little time they had left hit Bea like a blow to the stomach. 'My visa runs out in less than a month.' She took a deep breath. 'You would have to get someone new anyway for the rest of the time. Maybe it's better for you to do that sooner than later.'

'Yes, sure. You're right,' he said bleakly. 'I'll contact the agency tomorrow.'

There was a heavy silence. 'I wish I could stay,' said Bea wistfully, understanding now that it was too late just how much she was dreading having to leave.

'It doesn't matter.' Chase couldn't bear the thought that she might be trying to spare his feelings. He forced a smile. 'We've had a good time, haven't we?'

'Yes,' said Bea. 'We have.'

He came over and took her by the waist, needing to touch her, to hold her, while he could. 'We might as well make the most of the time we've got left, don't you think?'

Suddenly terrified that she might be about to cry, Bea put her arms around him and buried her face in his throat. 'Yes,' she said unsteadily, 'let's do that.'

Bea pressed her mouth into Chase's shoulder and spread her hand over his stomach. She could feel his chest rising and falling with each slow, steady breath. They had made love with a kind of desperation, losing themselves in touch and taste and the wild surge of sensation, making the world go away for a while.

But the world was still there when their heartbeats returned to normal at last. The world where at some point soon they were going to have to say goodbye.

She didn't want to go. Bea admitted it to herself as she lay entwined with Chase. She wasn't ready to be sensible again, not yet.

I'm not going to fall in love with you. How confidently she had said it! She had meant it, too, although now it seemed incredible that she hadn't known that of course she was going to fall in love with him. How could she *not* fall in love when her heart seemed to stop every time she looked at him? When his smile clogged the breath in her throat and the merest brush of his hand was enough to set her senses zinging and singing with delight?

So, yes, she'd fallen in love in spite of her best intentions. It wouldn't last. Bea could see that already. She wasn't a fool. They were too different, and they wanted different things. They had both made that clear from the start. *I'm looking for a suitable girl,* Chase had said. *I don't want to marry you. You don't belong, and you never will.*

No, this was just a holiday romance, a consuming passion that would burn out eventually in the face of humdrum reality. But, while it did last, shouldn't she make the most of it, as Chase had said? If she left now, while things were so good, she might spend the rest of her life regretting it, and turning Chase into a fantasy figure that would bear little relation to the real man. Wouldn't it be better to stay until the excitement had worn off and practicalities had taken over, until she could kiss and say good-bye without her heart breaking, and they could both walk away without regret?

There was only one way she could stay long enough for that to happen.

'Chase?'

He was quiet, thinking too. 'Yes?'

'Chase,' said Bea slowly, 'how would it be if I stayed until Nick and Georgie came home?'

Chase lifted himself up on one elbow and looked down at her. Her skin was luminous in the moonlight and her eyes were like dark, gleaming pools.

'I thought you had to leave Australia?'

'I would have to,' said Bea, 'unless...' She stopped, wondering how best to put it.

'Unless what?' he asked, and she took a breath.

'Unless we got married. Wait!' she hurried on, flinging out a hand to stop him before he could react. 'Wait, I know what you're going to say, but it wouldn't be like that. I said I didn't want to marry you and I don't. It would just be a temporary arrangement. We could divorce as soon as your brother came home.'

Chase's eyes narrowed. 'What would be the point of getting married, then?'

'It would mean I could stay in Australia.'

'Ah,' he said, his voice empty of expression.

He could see it from Bea's point of view, of course. No more visa hassles, no need to go back to London with its bitter memories and its awkward encounters. She could set up her business in Sydney, just the way she had wanted.

'What would I get out of it?' he asked after a moment.

'You wouldn't have to look for someone else to look after Chloe,' said Bea.

'Not much of a reason to get married, is it?'

'No.' Bea swallowed at the hard edge to his voice. She had gone about this all wrong. 'No, it isn't. I just thought…we've got something good,' she tried to explain.

'We both know it's not going to last,' she stumbled on. 'I'm a city girl. You want a country girl, and I'm never going to be that, just like you're never going to live in Sydney and do the kind of things I want to do. I don't want to stay for ever, Chase, but I don't want to go. Not yet.'

'I don't want you to go, either,' he admitted.

'There's no pressure,' Bea said, gaining confidence. 'If you don't want to risk marriage, I'll quite understand, and I'll go as soon as you find another cook.

'I don't want you to think I'm getting involved or anything,' she added carefully, suddenly nervous in case she scared him off by appearing too keen. She had heard enough about Chase's reaction to the English girls who built him up into a romantic figure and then fell for him. As she had done. 'It's just...'

'Just sex?'

Bea hadn't been going to put it quite like that, but wasn't that what it boiled down to? 'Yes,' she said. 'It's the same for both of us, isn't it?'

Chase lay down and stared at the ceiling. 'Right,' he said.

'Getting married...it wouldn't mean anything. I wouldn't touch any of your money. We could make it a proper agreement, if you wanted. There'd be no question of commitment...' Bea trailed off unhappily.

Well, what had he expected? Chase asked himself. A passionate declaration of love? She was being straight with him. She was right, too. They did want different things. Their relationship would never work in the long-term...but it was working so far. It was working fine.

If he married her, Bea would stay. Only for two months, perhaps, but that would be two months when he wouldn't have to come home to an empty house and an empty bed, two months when he wouldn't keep turning his head and expecting to see her, or reaching out in the morning and finding that she wasn't there.

Bea bit her lip as the silence lengthened.

'Look, forget it,' she blurted out at last. 'It was just an idea. I just thought it might be a convenient arrangement, that's all.'

Chase turned towards her, and when Bea saw the smile curling the corner of his mouth she nearly wept with relief. 'Convenient?' he repeated as he swept a possessive hand over the contours of her body, his smile deepening as she shifted in instinctive response to his touch. 'Who for?'

'For both of us,' said Bea, hope trickling into her heart at the undercurrent of laughter in his voice.

'I can see it would be convenient for *you*.'

'For you, too,' she said as her breath shortened. 'You won't have to waste time seducing a new cook!'

'Good point,' said Chase, pinning her beneath him and kissing the curve of her shoulder so that she shivered and squirmed deliciously.

'And then there would be other compensations, wouldn't there?' he suggested.

Bea wrapped herself around him, her hands moving hungrily over his warm, solid back. 'Oh, yes,' she sighed against his mouth, 'there would definitely be compensations for both of us!'

'I think you might have talked me into it,' he murmured back, and that was the last talking they did for a long time.

Much later, Bea was lying in his arms, her body throbbing contentedly. 'Are you sure?' she asked.

'I'm sure,' said Chase lazily. 'We'll get married with no commitments and no messy emotions, and we'll get divorced before we have time to drive each other mad. You get what you want, a visa, and I get to behave badly with an unsuitable girl before I settle down with someone sensible.' He turned his head on the pillow and grinned at her. 'The more I think about it, the more I think it's just what I want!'

CHAPTER EIGHT

CHASE found Bea picking lemons in the garden when he came back to the homestead the next morning after setting the men to work.

'I've been making a few calls,' he said as he came across the grass towards her, stopping to ruffle Chloe's hair on the way. 'We can get married in Townsville.

'I know too many people in Mackinnon,' he answered Bea's questioning look. 'It would turn into a circus if we tried to get married quietly there. Before we knew what had happened there would be parties, and questions about why we hadn't waited for Nick and Georgie, and it could get awkward when they find out we're getting divorced just a couple of months down the line.'

'Townsville sounds fine,' said Bea. She knew that she was the one who had first suggested a divorce, but Chase didn't need to go on about it.

'We should get the next mob of cattle through the yards by the end of the week, and there are no more guests booked in for a while, so we might as well go on Monday,' he was saying.

His eyes rested on his niece who was playing happily on the grass. 'We'll have to take Chloe with us,' he added, 'but it can't be helped. We might as well stock up on a few things while we're there, too. There's more choice than in Mackinnon. Make a list of anything you need— and don't forget toothpaste and more beer,' he remembered.

It was a new slant on a wedding list. 'Very romantic,' said Bea a little tartly, and he glanced at her, his pale eyes as startling as ever beneath his hat.

'It's not about romance, is it?'

'No,' she said, looking down at the lemons in her hands, 'of course not.'

She couldn't help remembering how she had planned her wedding to Phil. They hadn't got to the stage of issuing invitations, thank God. Phil had mocked her for wanting a traditional wedding in the local church, with a marquee in her parents' garden. It would have been a family affair, and that's what it had been in the end, although not exactly the way she had planned. The affair had been between Phil and her sister.

It had been obvious then why Phil had shown so little enthusiasm for her suggestions. He had kept saying that there was no hurry, that they were living together, and there was no point in rushing into an expensive wedding until they could afford it. Looking back on it, Bea could see that these had just been excuses, and that he hadn't been ready for marriage—at least, not to her.

And now she was contemplating marriage again. There would be no traditional wedding this time, just a brief ceremony, with no marquee, no guests, no family.

'What's the matter?' Chase was watching her more closely than she realised.

'Nothing. It's just not going to be how I always imagined my wedding, that's all.'

'It's not too late to change your mind,' he said.

Bea looked at him. He was standing a few feet away, every line of his body overwhelmingly distinct against the dazzling light. His shirt was open at the neck and, as her eyes drifted downwards, she imagined undoing the buttons, touching her lips to his bare chest, and she was shaken by a wave of lust that left her feeling dizzy and disorientated for a moment.

'Bea?'

Bea blinked the giddiness away. 'I don't want to change my mind,' she said.

'Sure?'

'Sure.'

'Come here.' Her hands were full of lemons, so Chase took her just above the elbows and drew her towards him to kiss her.

Bea felt the world shift beneath her feet. She had the strangest sensation, as if her whole life had been arrowing into the intensity of that moment, standing in the garden at Calulla Downs with the huge outback sky arching over her head. Chase's shirt smelt of hot, dry dust and sunlight and horses, mingled with the scent of the lemons in her hands.

'It will be worth it,' he said as he let her go.

Bea felt ridiculously close to tears, but she managed a smile. 'I know.'

They flew to Townsville four days later. Being in the plane again felt very strange to Bea. The last time, she had been nervous about entrusting herself to the grim stranger Chase had been, and she felt a very long way from home.

And now…now Chase was her lover, soon to be her husband, and she felt utterly safe in his hands. True, the outback still didn't feel like home, but at least it was not quite as alien as it had been. It wasn't really her kind of thing, of course, but if you liked starry nights and silence and spectacular sunsets, then there was no doubt that the outback was the place for you.

Not for her, of course. She was still an urban girl through and through, Bea reminded herself. She liked the bustle of the city, not the hush of the creek at dusk, but it didn't mean that she couldn't appreciate the bush…for a little while.

The truth, however, was that Bea didn't enjoy being back in a town quite as much as she had expected. It felt odd to be walking along pavements again, and she felt overwhelmed by the noise of the traffic, by the number of people, by the height of the buildings. And Townsville, busy though it was, was hardly Sydney or London. How on earth was she going to get on in a big city now?

But she didn't have to face the big city yet. She had two more months in the outback, two more months with Chase. And tomorrow she was getting married.

Bea felt her spirits rise as they left their things at the hotel and went out to lunch. Chloe clamoured to have a hamburger and chips, and although Bea was longing for some fish after the Calulla Downs diet of beef, beef and more beef, the little girl was so excited at the prospect that she gave in. They found a fast-food joint, where they were served a flaccid hamburger in a polystyrene box with dry, tasteless French fries.

Chloe thought it was delicious. 'I wish we could have this every day!'

Bea laughed. 'You'd soon get bored of it if you did.'

'I wouldn't!'

'Well, I'd get bored cooking it,' Bea told her.

'Will you make me a hamburger for my birthday?' Chloe asked.

'That depends when it is.'

'July the fifteenth. I'm going to be six,' she said proudly.

Bea's eyes flickered to Chase and then away. Chloe was thrilled at the idea of the wedding, and it seemed a shame to spoil her pleasure by telling her the truth, which was that Bea was unlikely to still be around on her birthday. The thought was like a cloud passing over the sun.

'We'll see,' she said, carefully non-committal.

'I guess you won't be serving hamburgers when you set up your catering business,' said Chase when Chloe was absorbed in sucking up the last of her milkshake.

He thought he had better reassure Bea that he hadn't forgotten her ambition. It was too easy to forget when she was sitting there with the sunlight in her golden eyes and glinting off her cloud of brown hair, when her face was warm and vivid, and the beautiful mouth was curved upwards into the smile that never failed to make his throat tighten.

Right then, Bea couldn't imagine cooking anywhere other than the kitchen at Calulla Downs, let alone setting up a business, but she didn't want Chase to think that she had forgotten their agreement. 'No, I'm strictly a canapé sort of cook,' she said lightly. 'The fiddlier the better.'

That ought to convince him that she had no intention of outstaying her welcome. There was no call for canapés at Calulla Downs.

After lunch, they went to buy a ring. Bea felt very awkward in the jeweller's shop, and selected the first plain gold band that fitted, but when she tried to pay for it herself, Chase wouldn't allow it.

'I'll dock it out of your wages,' he joked, handing over a credit card.

Short of having an unseemly tussle, Bea didn't see much option but to accept with good grace. 'Thank you,' she said, vowing to find some way to repay him before she went. She would be getting far more out of their marriage than he would, and it didn't seem fair that he should have to pay for everything, too.

There was a short silence while the assistant busied himself with the card. Bea picked up the ring in its box and pretended to admire it. 'It's lovely.'

'Want a diamond one to go with it?' said Chase.

Bea glanced at him uncertainly. Was this another joke? It was hard to tell from his expression. She attempted a laugh. 'Not if it's coming out of my wages too!'

'The diamonds would be on me.'

His voice was casual, but when their eyes caught, the look held, and for some reason Bea's heart started to slam uncomfortably against her ribs. She wrenched her gaze away with an effort.

'I had a diamond ring when I was engaged to Phil,' she told him. 'It didn't do me much good. I never made it to the wedding I planned then, so perhaps if I skip all the trimmings, it'll be second-time lucky.'

Chase's eyes rested on her averted face. 'I hope it will,' he said.

Chloe was in a fever of impatience to go and buy the dress she had been promised for the wedding, so Chase went off to deal with station business and left them to it. Bea had never shopped with a five-year-old before but, for a child who rarely saw more than the general store in Mackinnon, Chloe had a remarkably clear idea of what she wanted.

She set her heart on a pink, frilly confection that was so patently unsuitable for the outback that Bea looked at her with new interest.

'I think you might have the makings of a city girl,' she said, and bought her hairclips and a plastic necklace to match.

'What do you think I should wear?' she asked Chloe.

Chloe was keen on a long, white dress with a skirt like a meringue, which came complete with a tiara and a veil, but Bea didn't think Chase would appreciate the joke if she turned up in that.

'I suppose I *could* wear one of the dresses I've got with me,' she said. She didn't want to look as if she was making a big deal out of the wedding. On the other hand, she didn't have anything that would really be suitable, and it might look a bit odd if Chloe outshone her as the bridesmaid. It *was* her wedding, after all, and it might be the only one she ever had.

Fortunately, Chloe vetoed the suggestion that she should make do with what she had, and they had the perfect excuse to carry on shopping. In the end, Bea found a sleeveless raw silk dress in an unusual bronze that brought out the colour of her eyes, which she thought was suitably stylish without looking as if she was trying too hard. With it, she bought a straw boater and wonderful peep-toe shoes with perilous heels to remind herself of the girl she had once been.

The girl she still was, Bea corrected herself hurriedly.

Each secretly glad that they didn't have to wear the other's outfit, they decided to go and have a drink to celebrate their successful purchases. They found a café in the centre of town, and sat at a table outside under a parasol, where they could watch the world go by.

'What can I get you?' their waitress asked above them in a cheerful voice.

Cheerful, and very familiar.

Bea did a double take. 'Emily!'

'Bea!' Emily stared, just as surprised, and then, being Emily, homed in on a complete irrelevance. 'What's happened to your hair?' she demanded, eyeing Bea's curls with astonishment. 'Don't tell me your hair-dryer broke!'

Bea didn't feel like going into her changed attitude to her hair right then. 'Emily, what are you doing here?' she asked severely.

'What am *I* doing here? You were supposed to be in Sydney by now!'

'I thought *you* were setting up home with Baz!'

'Oh, that didn't work out,' said Emily with an airy gesture that dismissed Baz to the past. 'I was heading back to Sydney—to you!—and I stopped here on the way. I liked it, so I thought I would stay for a few weeks, earn enough money to learn to dive and then maybe head out to the reef.'

She tucked her order book into her apron pocket and fixed Bea with a beady look. 'So that explains why I'm here, but not why you're sitting here with your hair all frizzy!'

'It's not frizzy! It's just…easier to look after…like this.'

'Emily?' Chloe tugged at her apron, ignoring Bea's warning look. 'Bea and Chase are getting married tomorrow, and I'm going to be bridesmaid!'

'Sorry, I don't think I can have heard that right,' said Emily, shaking her head as if to clear her ear. 'I know you couldn't have said *Bea* was getting married—unless you mean another Bea? Because I used to have a friend called Bea, who wouldn't dream of getting married without telling me, so maybe you've muddled her up with someone else?'

Her sarcasm went over Chloe's head. 'No,' she said earnestly, 'it's this Bea.'

'*Bea?*' said Emily awfully.

'Well, you haven't been here to tell,' said Bea, on the defensive.

Emily was outraged. 'You mean it's true?'

'It's not quite how it seems—'

'*You* are marrying *Chase Sutherland*? When did this happen?'

'It's a bit difficult to explain at the moment,' said Bea, harried, indicating Chloe with her eyes. 'Why don't I meet you later?'

'Where are you staying?' Emily whistled when she heard. 'He's not paying for you, is he?'

'Is it expensive?' Bea looked anxious. She hadn't even thought about how much the hotel would cost. Perhaps she should have offered to pay for that instead of the ring?

'It's the best,' said Emily. 'Look, I finish here at six, so I'll meet you in the bar there at half past—and you'd better be ready to tell me *everything*! Now, how about some ice cream?'

she said in a different tone, and winked at Chloe. 'It's on the house!'

Chase was unsurprised to hear that Emily had moved on from Baz, and being ignorant of the rules of female friendship, didn't understand why Bea was in a tizzy about Emily discovering that she was actually getting married without having discussed it with her.

'She had to find out some time,' he pointed out reasonably. 'How else were you going to explain that you'd managed to stay in Sydney and set up a business out here?'

Bea didn't bother explaining to him that being reasonable wasn't the point of her friendship with Emily.

'I'll put Chloe to bed,' he offered. 'You go and have a drink with Emily.'

Emily was waiting for her at the bar. 'So, tell,' she ordered.

'There's not much to tell,' said Bea, slipping onto a stool next to her. She explained about Nick staying on in the States with Georgie, and her visa running out. 'Getting married is just a way of getting round regulations. It's all right for you, you can stay as long as you like.'

'But I thought you hated the outback!'

Bea's eyes slid away from Emily's. 'I'm not planning to stay. Chase and I have agreed, it's just a temporary arrangement. As soon as Nick and Georgie are back, I'll be off, but this time I will be able to stay in Sydney.'

'I can't believe it,' grumbled Emily. 'You're living my fantasy!'

'I thought your fantasy was living with Baz. What happened?'

Emily sighed. 'You were right, I got bored. At Calulla Downs, he was out all day, and we'd just have the evenings, but as soon as we were spending twenty-four hours a day together, we drove each other mad. Baz couldn't talk about anything except horses and cattle and when the next rodeo was.'

'So he didn't take you home?'

'Oh, yes, I met his parents, but they didn't have much to say for themselves, either. Where they lived wasn't romantic at all. It wasn't like Calulla Downs. It was just…boring. I didn't fit in at all. His parents thought I was weird for talking the whole time, and I think Baz was relieved in the end when I said I was leaving.'

'What are you going to do now?'

'I think I'll be a beach bum for a while,' said Emily gaily. 'Not that it stops me being insanely jealous of you!'

'You've got no need to be,' said Bea, fiddling with her glass. 'It's not as if we're really getting married.'

'You're getting a ring on *your* finger, aren't you? How much more married do you need to be?'

'Well, let's say we're not going to be living happily ever after,' said Bea with an unconscious sigh.

'That's up to you,' said Emily. She glanced at Bea. 'Are you sleeping with him?'

Bea's eyes wandered vaguely around the bar, and Emily sat back on her stool.

'Aha! You are! I always *thought* there was something between you and Chase!'

'It's not a big deal,' said Bea hastily.

'Well, make it a big deal!' said Emily. 'Come on, Bea! He can be a bit forbidding, I know, but he's not bad-looking, and he must be worth a bit. Imagine being mistress of all those acres!'

'He's not really my type,' muttered Bea.

'You wouldn't be sleeping with him if he wasn't your type,' Emily pointed out, and then her eyes narrowed in sudden comprehension. 'You're in love with him, aren't you?'

'No!' Bea almost shouted it. 'OK, I find him quite attractive,' she added more calmly, 'but it's just sex.' She was desperate to convince Emily that she wasn't serious about Chase, or perhaps she was desperate to convince herself. 'I've got no intention of being stuck out in the outback for ever,' she said loudly. 'I can't wait to get back to Sydney.'

'There's no need to shout, Bea, we all know that.' Chase spoke quietly right behind her, and she spun round on her stool. His expression was closed, his eyes shuttered. 'I'm sorry to disturb you, but Chloe's insisting you go up and say goodnight.'

Bea hesitated. She wanted to explain what he had heard, but what could she say? He wouldn't want to hear that she was in love with him. They were getting married the next day. It would be hard to find a surer way of making him feel trapped.

'I'll go up now,' she said awkwardly. 'See you later, Emily.'

But when she went down again, Emily had gone, and Chase was sitting on his own looking bleakly into a beer.

'Where's Emily?' she asked.

'She had to meet some diving instructor who I guess is Baz's replacement.'

'Did she say how I could get in touch with her?'

'No, but she's coming to the wedding to-morrow.'

Dismayed, Bea sat down next to him. She loved Emily, but she didn't trust her an inch. 'Didn't you tell her we didn't want to make a fuss?'

'I tried, but she insisted on coming to be your witness. I couldn't think of a good reason to refuse.'

His voice was pleasant, but distant and Bea's heart twisted. 'Chase—' she began impulsively, but he stopped her before she could go any further.

'You don't need to say anything, Bea,' he said. 'We both know what we agreed. We'll get married for two months, and where you want to go and what you want to do after that is entirely up to you.'

We're married! Bea looked at the ring on her finger, and tried to take it in. The ceremony itself had been a blur, and all she remembered was holding tightly to Chase's hand.

Chase had brought a posy of bush flowers for Chloe to give her that morning. Where the more usual roses would have been insipid with Bea's dress, the bouquet with its outback colours and dramatic shapes looked wonderful.

Bea was delighted. 'How did you know?' she asked him.

'I didn't,' said Chase. 'I just chose the ones that made me think of you.'

'They're beautiful,' she said and, as she kissed him on the cheek, she felt his arm close around her. The distance between them had dissipated in bed the night before, and they had reached a tacit agreement to make the most of the time they had together, without thinking about the future.

'Thank you,' she said softly in his ear.

Observing this, Emily had rolled her eyes. 'Oh, yes, *sure* you're not in love with him,' she muttered in an aside, but Bea chose not to hear. It was her wedding day, and she could do whatever she wanted.

It turned into a surprisingly happy day. Emily had brought her diving instructor with her. He bore a startling resemblance to Baz, and was so laid-back that he was practically horizontal.

'As soon as I saw him I fancied the pants off him,' Emily confided to Bea.

In spite of Chloe's pleas to return for hamburgers, they had lunch in a restaurant on the waterfront, and sat all afternoon in the dappled light of a pergola. Emily ordered champagne, and insisted on making a toast.

'To convenience!' she said ironically.

Bea was very aware of Chase beside her. Her husband. A temporary husband, maybe, but hers for the next two months.

Her hands twitched with the longing to reach out and touch him, and she had to clutch them together at times to stop them moving towards him of their own accord. She knew that she could touch him if she wanted to—he was her husband, after all—but she was afraid that the moment she laid a finger on him she would lose all vestiges of control, which might not go down too well with the other diners.

So she sat, smiling and chatting and simmering with desire, and longed for the night to come.

When Emily got reluctantly to her feet and said that she had to go, Bea put up only a token protest. Now all they had to do was get Chloe to bed.

Easier said than done. Chloe was thoroughly over-excited by the time they got back to the hotel, and refused point blank to take her dress off at first. 'I'm not tired,' she said mutinously. 'I don't want to go to sleep.'

When Bea finally persuaded her into bed, her eyelids were drooping with exhaustion. Bea kissed her goodnight and tiptoed through into the adjoining room, closing the connecting door softly behind her.

Chase was lying on top of the bed, his hands behind his head, and for a moment they just looked at each other. Then he smiled and lifted an arm invitingly.

Kicking off her shoes, Bea crawled onto the bed beside him and snuggled into his side.

'Well, we did it,' she said.

Chase lifted her hand and fingered the gold ring, picking his words with care. 'Was it hard for you today?' he asked. 'Thinking about what it would have been like if you'd got married as you planned?'

'No, it wasn't hard,' said Bea honestly. She rested her head on his chest, tired now that the day was over at last. 'If I'd married Phil, I would have spent my wedding day in a frenzy about place settings and food and whether the relatives were going to behave. As it was, we didn't have to worry about anything.

'It was the perfect wedding, in fact,' she told him, only half joking. 'Just the two of us, and no pressure.'

'No pressure...' Chase repeated thoughtfully. 'That had better be the motto of our marriage.'

'We could do worse.'

Rolling Bea beneath him with a smile, he bent to kiss her. 'Some things we could do better,' he said. 'If we practise...'

Bea's honeymoon, if it could be called that, was spent stocking up on fresh fruit and vegetables that they couldn't grow at Calulla Downs, loading it all into the plane and unloading it at the other end. By the time she had put everything away, she barely had five minutes to unpack before she was back in the kitchen, preparing the evening meal.

Her wedding ring seemed very shiny and obvious on her finger. Every time Bea moved her hand, it winked and gleamed in the light. She waited for the stockmen to comment on it, or to mention the fact that she and Chase had actually got married, but no! It was horses and cattle and how many points of rain they'd had, just as usual. Bea wondered whether they'd even noticed that she and Chase hadn't been there.

'Do they know we got married yesterday?' she asked Chase incredulously when the stockmen had trooped out to their own quarters.

Chase shrugged. 'I think so. I told Doug, anyway, when I explained that I'd be away for a couple of days.'

'I can't believe they didn't even acknowledge it!'

'What did you expect?' said Chase. 'A welcome home party with champagne and canapés?'

'A word of congratulation might have been nice,' she said a little sulkily.

'If you're looking for social skills, you've come to the wrong place,' he pointed out, dumping plates in the sink. 'Why do you want congratulations, anyway? It's not as if it's a real marriage.'

'Yes, but they don't know that!'

Chase sighed. 'Bea, what is the problem?'

What *was* the problem? Bea didn't know. She just knew that she felt grouchy and obscurely hurt by the stockmen's indifference, by their air of having seen girls like her come and go a thousand times. She wanted to shout at them and remind them that Chase hadn't married any of the others, he had married *her*.

It wouldn't have killed them to have welcomed her back, or at least pretended that she was more than just one in a very long line, would it? Bea thought, washing up huffily.

Another reason, if she needed one, why she would probably be delighted to leave at the end of two months. She belonged in a city, with the kind of people who would throw a party for you if they heard you'd just got married, and yes, there *would* be champagne and canapés! What was so wrong with that?

It didn't occur to Bea that the men might simply be shy, or intimidated by her assurance. She saw their lack of response as a challenge. They obviously thought that she would never belong in the outback, and that there was no point in wasting any of their rare words on someone who would inevitably leave, wedding ring or no wedding ring.

Now Bea was on her mettle. She might not be intending to stay in the outback for ever but, as she had pointed out to Chase, the stockmen weren't to know that.

Her chin lifted, and her eyes held a militant sparkle. She would show those men that she wasn't just the silly city girl they so obviously thought her, and that she was quite capable of belonging if she wanted to. And when she *did* leave, she vowed, they would miss her!

Determined to get the hang of this outback business, Bea made Chase take her riding again that Saturday, and bravely refused the leading rein. She even managed a brief, and exceedingly uncomfortable, trot, and when Chase suggested a canter, she was so excited and pleased with herself for not falling off, that he laughed.

'We'll have you rodeo riding next!' he said, helping her out of the saddle.

'I think I'll leave the bucking broncos to you,' said Bea, but she couldn't help feeling thrilled by his approval.

Pathetic, really. She was glad Emily wasn't there to see how a mere word of praise from Chase made her quite light-headed with pleasure.

Of course, trundling a few yards on placid old Duke wouldn't be enough to get her accepted by these hard-riding men, but it was a start, wasn't it?

Encouraged, she began to listen intently to their talk about mustering and bull-catching and horse-breaking in the hope that she might be able to join in one day without Chase having to act as an interpreter, but it was all pretty baffling still, she had to admit.

What she needed, Bea decided, was go down to the cattle yards and see the men at work. She had only the haziest idea of what they actually did down there, but she could see herself leaning on the rails, perhaps slapping the rump of a cow every now and then.

'Fattening up nicely!' she would call out to the stockmen.

Or would that sound a bit heartless?

Maybe it would be better if she noticed that someone had forgotten to close a gate or something? She wouldn't make a fuss, she would just shut it quietly, but Chase would notice, of course. He would smile his thanks, and afterwards he would say what a good thing it was that she'd been there.

'You'd better come down to the yards more often,' he would say. 'The boys were just saying how nice it was to have you around.'

After this pleasant daydream, the reality of the cattle yards came as a terrible shock. Bea managed to pick a day when they were dehorning calves. There was blood spurting everywhere, and the press of cattle bellowing and milling around in clouds of dust made her nervous. She hadn't realised that cows could be that big or look that wild.

She certainly wouldn't be slapping any rumps, thought Bea, edging away. So much for her daydream!

On the other hand, wasn't that a gate over there, standing wide open? If they didn't watch out, all those cattle in the holding paddock would be making a break for it. Bea trotted over.

'What the hell are you doing?' Chase came galloping up through the dust on a huge, snorting horse. 'We're just about to drive that lot through here!' He wheeled the horse around with an iron hand. 'Get out of the way!' he shouted over the sound of the bellowing animals. 'And don't come out again without a hat!'

Mortified, Bea beat a hasty retreat to the homestead. Sometimes it seemed that the more she tried, the less she fitted in. When they ran low on flour, she decided to drive into Mackinnon with Chloe and go to the local store rather than wait for the weekly delivery. Because that was the kind of thing country girls did, right?

She forgot that country girls knew how to use the four-wheel drive. The track was far rougher than Bea had imagined, and she was about halfway between the homestead and the sealed road—in other words, a long way from anywhere—when she drove into sand and was promptly bogged. She had to get Chloe to show her how to use the radio and call Chase up for help.

He came, but he was in the middle of a particularly busy day, and not best pleased, to put it mildly.

That night, they went to bed in grim silence. Chase lay very still, but Bea knew that he wasn't sleeping either.

'I'm sorry,' she said miserably into the darkness at last.

There was a pause, and then he sighed. 'It's my fault,' he said. 'I can't expect you to know about driving on these roads. You've probably never been off a sealed road before.'

He made it sound extraordinary, as if there weren't millions and millions of perfectly good drivers like her who never needed to venture off tarmac. Bea knew that he was trying to comfort her, but it just made her feel even more of an outsider.

'No,' she agreed dully.

'I'm sorry I shouted at you.'

When she didn't respond, Chase rolled over and kissed her shoulder, working his slow, seductive way along to her throat. Even depressed as she was, Bea couldn't prevent an instinctive shudder of response and, without meaning to, she lifted her arms to encircle his back and pull him closer.

'We've both had a bad day,' he murmured against her warm skin. 'Let's make it a good night, and forget about it.'

This was the only place she belonged, thought Bea later, lying sleepy and replete in Chase's arms. With her body still thrilling from his touch, it seemed enough, but they couldn't spend their whole time in bed, as Emily and Baz had discovered. Chase might want her here right now, but he was a tough, shrewd man with a strong practical streak, and he had never pretended to be anything else. A wife who couldn't even drive into town to do the shopping without having to be rescued was no use to him. He needed a woman who would be a partner, not a liability.

She had better not forget that, Bea told herself sternly, because Chase certainly wouldn't.

CHAPTER NINE

AND just in case he needed reminding, Erin arrived two days later.

Erin, it turned out, was Georgie's cousin. She and her husband ran a place in New South Wales, Chase explained when he came back from answering the phone with the news that there would be another two for supper the following night. They would be spending a couple of days at Calulla Downs on their way to buy bulls' semen or something at a station near Tennant Creek.

Bea never understood exactly what they were doing, and she was damned if she was going to ask. From the moment Erin arrived, stepping out of their big four-wheel drive in jeans and an authentic Akubra, she made Bea feel utterly inadequate.

She might have been designed to show Chase the kind of woman he really needed. Out all day with the men, at supper she joined in their discussions about bore holes and salt licks and the price of feed, and was instantly accepted as someone who knew what she was talking about.

Tall and slim, she looked wonderful in jeans and a shirt, and raised her eyebrows at Bea's habit of changing into a dress every evening.

'You can tell *you* didn't grow up in the outback!' she said with a light laugh.

It was clear that she herself wouldn't have been seen dead in anything so frivolous and impractical. Eyeing her sourly, Bea guessed that no lipsticks cluttered Erin's bathroom. She couldn't imagine Erin squeezing her feet into high-heeled shoes and convincing herself that they fitted just because they were the only size available, or beginning her packing with a travel hair-dryer.

Why would she bother, after all? Her hair was cut short and stylishly practical, and with those sickeningly long legs she had no need of any extra inches. She was annoyingly attractive as she was, with healthy skin, good bones and beautiful green eyes that held a distinctly chilly expression whenever they rested on Bea, who took to drying her hair in its sleek, time-consuming style again out of sheer contrariness. There was no way she could compete with Erin in the suitability stakes, so she might as well not try!

That was obviously Erin's opinion too. Her attitude to Bea was amused and faintly patronising. She spotted the wedding ring on Bea's finger straight away—she wasn't *that* unfeminine—and when Chase introduced Bea as his wife, she didn't bother to conceal her amazement.

'You're *married*?' She didn't actually add *Why*? but she might as well have done.

'I'm sorry if I seemed surprised,' she explained to Bea later, when she had deigned to offer her some help in the kitchen. 'We'd all given up on Chase getting married. We never thought he would get over Georgie marrying Nick.

'Oh!' Erin put a hand to her mouth in a bad pretence at dismay. 'I haven't said anything I shouldn't, have I?'

Bea, chopping onions, set her teeth. 'It's all right, Chase told me all about Georgie,' she said evenly.

'Then you'll know how much he adored her?'

Bea's fingers tightened around the knife. 'Yes, but then I've always thought that it's better to be a last love than a first love.'

'You're a brave woman then.' Erin offered a bright, insincere smile. 'Georgie's a hard act for any girl to follow.'

Bea appreciated the slight stress on that 'any'. No need for Erin to add, 'especially one like you.'

'I remember how jealous I was of her when we were kids,' Erin was saying. Bea had given her some tomatoes to slice, and it was an eye-opener to see what a botch someone could make of such a simple job. 'Georgie wasn't just pretty, she was a fantastic rider. You'd never think it to look at her now, but she could ride before she could walk.'

Erin paused delicately. 'Do you ride, Bea?'

'Occasionally,' said Bea with defiance, thinking of her ambles on Duke. And she *had* cantered. Cantering was riding, wasn't it?

'Oh.'

It was perfectly judged, managing to suggest just the right level of polite disbelief mingled with regretful bewilderment. Why on earth, Bea could practically hear Erin thinking, had Chase tied himself up with a girl like this?

Erin reached for another tomato. 'I gather you're a very good cook,' she said, managing to make just as much of a botch up of that one too.

Bea had no trouble in interpreting this. Chase had only married her because of her way with gravy and apple pies.

Her smile glittered quite as falsely as Erin's. 'Yes, Chase loves my cooking,' she said soulfully, 'among other things, of course!'

Erin looked down her nose with distaste. Evidently real outback women didn't go in for suggestive remarks.

'He says you're from London.' She made it sound like Pluto. 'You must miss the bright lights.'

In other words, get back to where you belong, Bea translated sourly.

'Not at all,' she declared, lifting her chin.

But, much as she hated to admit it, Erin's barbed comments had had an effect.

Why was she wasting her time trying to be accepted out here? It was obvious that she was never going to belong. Chase had told her that himself not so long ago. She could spend a lifetime learning how to lasso calves and wield a branding iron, reflected Bea, but the likes of Erin would always think of her as a London girl in a dress, out of place and out of her depth.

She didn't even know if Chase wanted her to stay. When he made love to her, it was hard to believe that he didn't feel something, but he was careful to let no words that might smack of commitment past his lips. He seemed happy to accept the situation as it was, and not think about the future.

She should do the same.

Bea thought about it as Erin went off to join the men on the veranda for a beer, obviously considering that she had done enough woman's work in the kitchen.

Had she fallen into the classic trap of confusing lust with love? Bea paused in the act of scraping Erin's ruined tomatoes into a pot to make a sauce and frowned.

She had often accused Emily of doing the same thing, and now it was looking suspiciously as if she had fallen for the same romantic dream. Why else would she have started dreaming about helping out in the yards or galloping confidently around the outback?

Did she really think Chase could be that easily fooled into wanting to spend the rest of his life with her?

Bea cringed inwardly when she thought of how obvious her attempts to fit in must have seemed to Chase. She had let herself get carried away by the intensity of their physical attraction, forgetting that they had little else in common.

The sensible side of Bea's nature reasserted itself with relief after weeks of being ignored.

Really, what had she been thinking of? Had she honestly imagined that she could be happy boiling billies and chasing cows around the outback?

The only trouble was that now she couldn't imagine being happy without Chase.

Well, there was no hurry, Bea told herself sensibly. Nick and Georgie weren't due back for another three weeks at least. Time enough to think about whether her feelings for Chase were real or just romantic dreams dressing up plain, unadulterated lust.

In the meantime, she should relax and enjoy what she and Chase had without trying to pretend that she was someone she wasn't. She would be herself and if Erin and the stockmen didn't like it, that was just too bad.

'How would you like a day out?'

It was nearly a week later when Chase came in from the office and found Bea studying a recipe for apple cobbler. A thousand ways to cook stodge, she and Emily had called it when they found the cookbook, yellow with age, tucked away on a shelf in the corridor, and Bea was a little embarrassed to find herself poring over it for inspiration more and more often.

'A day out?' she repeated blankly, images of ice creams and funfairs chasing bizarrely around her brain. 'Where?'

'I've just been talking to the land agents in Mackinnon,' said Chase. 'There's a property for sale on the other side of town.'

Bea sat back, putting a finger in the book to keep her place. 'Are you thinking of buying it?'

'I might go and have a look,' he said. 'I just wondered if you wanted to come with me.'

'Me?'

The sensible side of Bea, having recovered its ascendancy over the last few days, instantly urged caution. Things had been much better between them since she had stopped trying to pretend that she would ever fit in, but it might also have had something to do with the fact that Chase had been so busy outside that they had hardly spent any time alone.

Except when they were in bed, where there was never any problem about getting on.

'I wouldn't know the first thing about buying a station,' said sensible Bea, even as the reckless romantic who had emerged so alarmingly recently was thrilling at the mere thought of going anywhere with him.

'That doesn't matter,' said Chase. 'We could make a day of it. I'm sure Julie wouldn't mind looking after Chloe, just this once, and it would make a change for you,' he went on, uneasily aware of how much he wanted Bea to come with him.

And, uneasily aware of how she wanted to go, Bea said that she would. Only because she couldn't think of a good reason to refuse, sensible Bea justified it to herself.

The other, dangerous, Bea, didn't bother with reasons or excuses. She was just standing there and smiling, while her body cheered at the prospect of a whole day alone with him.

Sensible Bea was firmly back in control, however, by the time they flew over to look at the station Chase was thinking of buying. She was getting used to jumping into a plane the way most people got into a car.

'What's this place called?' she asked, settling into her seat.

'Wilbara.' Chase eased the joystick back as the plane levelled off. 'I can just remember it being a fair-size station before it was gobbled up by a conglomerate with two other properties. They ran cattle on the land, but abandoned the homestead and the yards. Nothing much has been done on the property for years. It's a shame, because it's good grazing land over there.'

They had been flying for about three quarters of an hour when Chase swooped down to have a closer look at the ground. 'This ought to be Wilbara now,' he said.

Bea peered out of her window, wondering how on earth he could tell. It looked exactly the same to her, a bit rockier maybe, but otherwise indistinguishable from the land, rough and red with a sparse scattering of grey-green scrub, that stretched out in a dizzying expanse to the curve of the earth.

'*That* is good grazing ground?' she said before she could help herself.

'We don't do lush green fields like you do in England,' said Chase with a sardonic look.

'You can say that again!'

'You should see it after the Wet,' he told her, banking the plane so that they flew along the line of the creek. 'If we get good rains, the grass will be over your head.'

Bea tried to picture the cracked red earth covered with a mantle of long grass, but she had to shake her head in defeat. 'I can't imagine it.'

'It's beautiful then,' said Chase warmly. 'You've never seen anything like it.'

'It sounds amazing.'

That was his chance to say that she could see it for herself if she wanted to stay for a few months longer, or to suggest that he would like to show her the miraculous transformation of the landscape but, if Chase was aware of his cue, he missed it.

Studying the ground below, he only grunted absently. 'It is,' was all he said.

Bea was furious with herself for being disappointed. She was supposed to be living for the present, enjoying their relationship while it lasted, and not wondering why he wasn't planning on spending the Wet with her.

'You'll have to send me a photo,' she said in a brittle voice.

Chase glanced at her sharply, but she had turned away and was making a pretence of watching two kangaroos loping through the scrub below them.

'Sure,' he said flatly.

Wilbara's airstrip was little more than a rough clearing in the bush. A bumpy landing in more ways than one, thought Bea, feeling as if she had been brought abruptly down to earth by Chase's blunt reminder that her time as his wife was strictly limited.

A wild-looking character who introduced himself as Wal was there to meet them.

'The agents said you'd be coming to have a look today,' he said laconically, and jerked his head in the direction of a battered ute. 'They thought you might want a vehicle, so I said I'd show you round.'

The three of them got into the front of the truck. Chase stretched an arm along the back of the bench seat and turned slightly so that he could talk to Wal, who set off at a cracking pace across the rough ground. Stuck in the middle on the slippery seat, Bea was lurched and jolted between the two men.

'Sorry,' she muttered, having been flung against Wal.

'Don't apologise,' he leered. 'I haven't had a pretty girl throwing herself at me for a long time!'

Edging back towards Chase, Bea could believe it. Wal might have been keeping an eye on things since the station closed down, but washing was evidently not high on his priority list.

She was appalled when she learnt that he had been left on his own. 'Don't you get lonely?' she said, wincing at the sound of her prim, prissy voice next to Wal's slow drawl. It was as if everything today was conspiring to remind her how English and out of place she was.

'Nah,' said Wal.

'But what do you do all day?'

'Shoot roos mostly.' He gave her a gap-toothed grin. 'I just *love* killing wildlife!'

Bea smiled nervously. She wasn't quite sure what to make of Wal, and it was obvious that the feeling was mutual.

'You two been married long?' he asked, with a curious look at Chase. He might as well have wondered out loud what Chase was doing with a wife like Bea.

'No, not long.'

Bea wished Wal would look where he was going. They were careering across the bush with a fine disregard for the fact that the ground was littered with rocky outcrops, scrubby trees and bleached wood. Wal would drive straight towards whatever was in his way, only swerving at the very last second.

'I was married once,' he said, avoiding a towering termite mound by inches. He screwed up his face in an effort of memory. 'What was her name now?'

By the end of the afternoon, Bea had been jolted and jarred over miles. Every now and then, Wal would pull up with a screech, and they would get out. Bea stood rubbing her aching bottom and waving the flies from her face while Chase and Wal inspected dams or studied the stray cows that had evidently escaped the last muster and were now running wild. They lifted their heads to eye the humans warily before turning and blundering off into the bush, just in case.

The cattle looked all right to Bea's inexperienced eye, but even she could see that otherwise Wilbara was in an appalling condition. The fences were broken and the dams and bore holes badly neglected. Still, she stared in disbelief when they returned to the airstrip and she saw Chase shaking Wal's hand in an unmistakable gesture of farewell.

'We're going?'

'I thought you'd be pleased,' said Chase, having heard her muttering under her breath every time they bounced over a particularly deep hole.

'You haven't even looked at the homestead!' Bea pointed out incredulously, and his heart sank. He had been afraid that she would think of that.

'I don't think it'll be up to much,' he said, taking her arm and urging her towards the plane.

Bea shook herself free. 'But that's where—' she stopped herself from saying 'we' just in time '—where *you'll* be living if you buy Wilbara. I can't believe you wouldn't even bother to look at it!'

'Want to see the homestead?' Wal offered obligingly.

'I don't think we'll bother,' Chase began, but Bea spoke firmly over him.

'Yes, please, Wal. We *would* like to see it.'

Wal beamed and opened the door of the ute. 'Hop in, then.'

He drove them down a rough track and pulled up with a flourish outside the homestead. 'There you go,' he said. 'Welcome to Wilbara.'

For several minutes, Bea could only stare in appalled silence. Once, perhaps, it had been a fine, solid building with a wide veranda, but now it was crumbling and neglected. The corrugated iron roof was hanging off the veranda in sheets, and the doors stood broken on their hinges.

To Bea, used by now to the gracious homestead at Calulla Downs with its polished wood and cool, luxuriant garden, it looked dismal and depressing, standing in a bare, dusty yard with a clutter of ramshackle huts behind it and not a blade of green to soften the view.

Inside, it was even less inviting. As they walked through, they left footprints in the thick layer of dust that lay over everything. Wal led them down a long corridor, enjoying his new role as a real estate agent.

Flinging open a door, he nudged Bea so hard that she nearly fell into the room. 'The passion pit!' he announced.

'What?'

He grinned. 'Master bedroom to you,' he told her with a lewd wink. 'All you need is a bed in here and you'll be well away!'

Bea coloured but Chase only asked how many bedrooms there were altogether.

'Six or seven, I reckon,' said Wal, having given the matter some thought. 'They had big families in those days, and no shortage of space. You two planning on having children?' he asked with frank curiosity.

'Not right at this moment,' said Chase, with a glance at Bea's hot face. No prizes for guessing that having a family was the *last* thing on her mind just then!

'Plenty of time for practising, eh?' Wal chuckled dirtily and ambled off down the corridor.

'Who *is* this guy?' hissed Bea at Chase as they made to follow him.

'He's just trying to wind you up,' said Chase dismissively.

'Well he's doing a very good job!'

'Ignore him.'

Easy for *him* to say. He hadn't been leered at all afternoon, and if Wal dug his elbow into her ribs one more time, she would punch him. Her side was black and blue as it was.

Bea peered into another gloomy room. 'God, what a dump!'

'You were the one who wanted to see it,' Chase pointed out irritably.

'Yes, and it's just as well I did, isn't it?' She flicked a switch on the wall to see if a little light might improve matters, but nothing happened.

'There's no electricity,' Wal informed them, popping up behind her. 'You could fix up the generator if you wanted,' he added, managing to suggest that needing electricity ranked somewhere up there with bathing in asses milk or peeling grapes as far as priorities went.

'Oh, we'd need the generator, darling,' said Bea naughtily. Wal wasn't the only one who could do winding up. 'You *know* I have to be able to plug in my hair-dryer!'

Wal thought that was a great joke. 'Hair-dryer!' he repeated, laughing wheezily, and Bea could hear him still chuckling as he took Chase outside to look in the tumbledown sheds around the yard.

Bea wandered back along to the kitchen. Having a wife who actually dried her hair probably counted as a guilty secret around here. She hoped Wal told everybody and ruined Chase's reputation. She wasn't invited to hang around and see the Wet, so what did she care?

She stood in the middle of the dusty floor and looked around the kitchen. It was a shame everything was so filthy, because now she looked at it properly, she could see that it had quite a lot of potential. Swept and scrubbed and with that dreary paint stripped off the walls, it would be a pleasant, decent-sized room. You could even knock through to the dining room next door and screen off the veranda there to make an eating area as at Calulla Downs, and if you put in some plants and a pergola it would make the whole kitchen a light and airy place to work.

Bea turned slowly in the dust, picturing herself there. It would need to be gutted completely, of course, and you'd have to get rid of those units and replace the sink… Her eye ran along the worktop, mentally replacing it with something cool and clean, and then came to a jarring halt.

What was that?

What *was* that?

'Oh—my—God!' croaked Bea.

A spider so enormous that her gaze had travelled over it uncomprehendingly at first before jerking back in disbelief was squatting evilly by a rusty old breadbin. It was the size of a man's hand, at least, with feet like boxing gloves.

All eight of them.

Horror gripped Bea by the throat and the hairs rose on the back of her neck. For a long moment she could only stare at the spider, paralysed by panic, and then as if sensing her fear, it scuttled forward.

Bea's scream would have done justice to any horror movie.

The spider stopped on the edge of the unit. Bea couldn't actually see its eyes, but it seemed to her that it was regarding her with a cold, unwavering stare. Very, very slowly, she began to edge backwards towards the door—there was no way she was turning her back on that thing!—only to scream again as she bumped into Chase who came running into the room.

'What is it?' he demanded urgently.

Bea clutched at him. 'S-s-sp-pp...' was all she could get out, and Chase followed the direction of her shaking finger.

'For God's sake, Bea, it's just a spider!'

Chase was clearly not in the mood to play the comforting hero. He took Bea's hands off him impatiently.

'He's a big fella, though, isn't he?' Wal had appeared now, and was studying the spider with admiration. 'Take a look at those paws on him!'

'Don't touch it!' shrieked Bea as Wal peered closer.

'Stop making such a fuss!' said Chase shortly. 'It's not going to hurt you.'

'It might go for Wal! Look at it, it's getting ready to jump.'

'Don't be ridiculous! Spiders don't attack without provocation.'

'Sometimes they do,' Wal joined in the argument. 'I knew a fella once opened a drawer and a big monster like this jumped up and bit him on the face.' Wal spread his fingers and clapped a hand over his face in graphic illustration. 'Spoilt his weekend,' he added with masterly understatement.

Bea moaned. 'I feel sick.'

'Pull yourself together,' Chase ordered, propelling her outside. 'You're being hysterical.'

He was so unsympathetic that Bea, who had been on the verge of tears, pulled herself free and glared at him. Whatever happened to love and protect? Any decent husband would have swept his wife into his arms and begged her to tell him that she was all right, not marched her outside and told her to stop making a fuss! He would have tackled the monster himself just to prove his love for her, instead of letting Wal— Wal!—be the hero.

Of course, any decent husband loved his wife, and Chase didn't do that. She kept forgetting.

From inside the kitchen came sounds of banging and thumping. It sounded as if a huge fight was going on. Bea looked nervously at the door.

'Do you think Wal is all right?'

'What, you think the spider's into kung fu?' asked Chase sarcastically.

'You can't tell with something like that. This is how horror films start, you know.' Bea hugged her arms together, feeling twitchy. 'Three people and a spider, alone, miles from help, and the next thing you know there's only two...'

Her imagination was leaping ahead, already seeing the spider, grotesquely enlarged, poking one of its assorted huge, hairy legs around the door, raking the veranda in frustration as it tried to drag her and Chase into its gaping fangs. All they would find later would be a few crushed bones. No one would ever know what had happened to her.

'Oh, God,' she whimpered, heedless of Chase's look of disgust, and when a moment or two later Wal appeared in the doorway, she was so relieved that she practically threw her arms around his neck.

'Are you all right, Wal?'

'Yeah, I'm all right,' he said, grinning broadly. 'The spider's not feeling too good.'

'Oh, *thank* you!'

'No worries,' said Wal. 'I told you I liked killing wildlife!'

Bea couldn't wait to get back to the plane. 'Are you sure you don't want to come with us?' she asked Wal, who looked surprised at her concern.

'Nah, I'll be right,' he said, apparently unperturbed at the prospect of sleeping and eating with spiders lurking all around him.

He waved at Bea as she climbed into the plane. 'See you next time,' he called after her.

'*Next time*?' said Bea to Chase as they strapped themselves in. 'He's got to be kidding!'

'Why?'

She gaped at him. 'You're not seriously thinking of coming back here?'

'I don't see why not. It's good land.'

'It's heaving with monstrous creatures!'

Chase sucked in his breath irritably. Why did she always have to exaggerate? 'It was only a spider,' he said, holding on to his temper with difficulty.

'That was not a spider,' said Bea. 'That thing had a starring role in *Arachnophobia*!'

'In what?'

'It's a film, a horror movie.' She sighed. 'But of course, you won't have seen it. You don't have cinemas, and anyway, why would you need to go and see a horror movie when you can live the horror right here at home!'

Chase swore under his breath. He should never have taken Bea to Wilbara. He had known that she would be horrified by the state of the house. It was one of the reasons why he hadn't wanted her to see it. He'd *told* her the homestead had been abandoned. Why had she had to insist on seeing it for herself?

And then that bloody spider had turned up.

She would never consider living there now.

Perhaps it was just as well. The whole idea had been stupid, Chase realised, scowling at the controls.

Even before she reacted so hysterically to that spider, it had been obvious that there was no way he could ever take a girl like Bea to Wilbara. A girl who fussed with her hair and wore ridiculous shoes and scattered garnish on her stews. It would have been a disaster.

It was just that he had wanted to take her to Wilbara, so that he could imagine her there when she was gone.

And she would go. Chase had known that all along. He had kept thinking, hoping, that she would adapt and learn to love the outback, and then he would go home and she would be doing something bizarre like painting her toenails.

At Wilbara she wouldn't even have a cooker she could switch on without the generator, and that was broken like everything else.

He could have Wilbara, but if he did he would never have Bea.

'You're not really thinking of buying that place, are you?' Bea broke into his thoughts.

'It's Wilbara, or stay on at Calulla Downs with Nick and Georgie,' he said curtly.

'But you can't live at a place like Wilbara on your own,' she objected.

Chase wished she would stop rubbing in the fact that she wouldn't be there to help him. He had already got that particular point.

'I won't be on my own,' he said shortly. 'I'll have stockmen who aren't so fussy about conditions. They don't need to wash their hair every day—unlike some people,' he couldn't resist adding.

'You should offer a job to Wal, then. He certainly doesn't wash every day!'

'I was going to do that anyway,' said Chase. 'He knows the land and he knows cattle. He'd be a useful person to have around.'

Unlike her. Why didn't he come right out and say it?

Bea hunched a shoulder angrily. 'Well, if you want to spend your life in a dump being stalked by giant spiders, I should go ahead and put in an offer. Wilbara's perfect for you!'

'What is it to you, anyway?' retorted Chase, nettled. 'You're not going to be there,' he reminded her brutally.

'No, I most certainly won't be there,' she told him. 'I'll be in Sydney, enjoying quaint little features like running water and telephones and electricity at the flick of a switch, and as I garnish my canapés I'll think of you cooking in that kitchen—because it *will* be you doing the cooking. You'll never get anyone to work for you in those conditions!'

There was a tight look around Chase's mouth. 'Maybe I'll get married,' he said unpleasantly. 'I'll find someone who's not afraid to get her hands dirty, and wants to work with me to build something good together, someone who doesn't go to pieces at the sight of a spider and wants to do something more with her life than fiddle around with fancy food for people who've got nothing better to do than stand around at parties bitching about each other.'

'Good idea,' said Bea, white with anger and hurt, 'except for the minor matter that you're already married!'

'Not for much longer,' he practically snarled back. 'Nick and Georgie should be back soon. We agreed that we would divorce then.'

'There's no need to panic, I'm not going to contest it in the hope that you'll sweep me off to Wilbara and hand me a dustpan and brush!'

'I never thought you would.'

'The sooner we get a divorce the better as far as I'm concerned.' Bea was too hurt to think about what she was saying. 'You might have to be a little less picky when it comes to a wife for Wilbara, though. Perhaps you should try advertising?' she suggested bitterly. '*Wanted: a wife, preferably spider lover, likes cleaning houses but not self.* I'm sure Erin could put you in touch with someone suitable!'

'Funny you should say that,' said Chase, baring his teeth. 'Erin said when she was here that she knew a girl she thought I'd get on with. That's one of the reasons she was disappointed to find that I'd married you. Apparently the girl is the daughter of one of Erin's neighbours, so she's grown up on a station.'

'She sounds just what you need,' said Bea with a glittering smile. 'Don't mind me, give her a ring when you get back!'

'Maybe I will.'

They didn't say a word to each other for the rest of the flight. Chase had left the car parked in the shade, and Bea banged the door behind her as she got in. Chase hated it when she did that.

Serve him right.

They were both so angry that neither noticed a spanking new vehicle parked by the veranda at the homestead. Bea jumped out and slammed her door again childishly before stalking towards the steps without a backward look. Chase was left to vent his fury on the car by slamming his door even louder.

'Bea, Bea!' Chloe danced out onto the veranda to meet her. 'Guess who's here?'

Bea halted. Wasn't Chloe supposed to be with Julie?

'What are you—' she began, but Chase was already looking behind her to the woman coming out of the homestead with her famous wide smile.

'Georgie!'

Ever afterwards, Bea only retained snapshot impressions of the next few minutes. She remembered looking at Chase and seeing the way the bitter, closed expression he had worn with her was lit by a smile that tore at her heart. Georgie, throwing herself into his arms for an uninhibited hug. Chloe's excited face.

And the stain on the side of the corrugated iron water tank that she stared at, her anger swamped by sudden desolation. Georgie was back, and now she would have to leave.

CHAPTER TEN

I'M NOT ready, she thought in panic. Of course she wanted to go, especially after today. Just not yet.

'And you must be Bea!' Georgie seized her hands with a dazzling smile. 'I can't thank you enough for looking after Chloe so well!'

Somehow Bea found herself swept into the homestead on the tide of Georgie's warmth. She hadn't wanted to like Georgie, and mentally dug in her heels to resist her charm, but it was no good. Georgie was simply impossible to dislike, just as Chase had said.

Disorientated, Bea shook her head to try and clear it. One minute she and Chase had been in the middle of a bitter fight, and the next they were being hugged and kissed and greeted excitedly.

Now Georgie was introducing her to Nick, who was every bit as attractive as Emily had said. He had twinkling eyes, a deep lazy voice, and a way of looking at you that made you feel that he had waited his whole life to meet you.

In short, he wasn't anything like Chase. Bea sneaked a glance between the two men. It has hard to believe that they were brothers. Next to Nick's effortless good looks and easy charm, Chase looked grimly reserved. A muscle was jumping in his clenched jaw and there was a tight look around his eyes.

'So you're my new sister-in-law,' said Nick, grinning as he held Bea at arm's length to study her. 'We've been hearing *all* about you!'

His warm appreciation seemed to annoy Chase, who turned to Georgie with a frown. 'What are you doing here?'

Georgie looked surprised at his tone, as well she might, Bea reflected, given the way Chase had been hugging her only a minute ago.

'I'd finished filming, and Nick and I were just about to leave for the second honeymoon we'd promised ourselves in Mexico when I had the most extraordinary phone call from my cousin Erin. She said you'd got married!' Georgie's green eyes widened. 'Well, we knew you wouldn't have done that without telling us unless something was wrong, and I was afraid it might be something to do with Chloe.'

'Why didn't you ring?' said Chase irritably. 'We could have told you Chloe was perfectly all right.'

'We did try and call you, but we couldn't get a reply, and then I got into a panic and insisted that we came straight back. I was in a fret all the way! I nearly had a fit when we got here and there was nobody around,' Georgie confided, 'but then we found Chloe when we went to find out whether Julie knew what was going on, and Chloe told us that you and Bea were in love, which was a huge relief, I can tell you, after some of the things Erin had been saying!'

Whoops, Chase wasn't going to like *that!*

He didn't. 'Chloe said *what?*'

'I told Mum I saw you and Bea kissing,' said Chloe pertly. 'And I showed her my bridesmaid's dress.'

'Why don't I go and put the kettle on?' said Bea, finding her voice quickly as Chase's mouth tightened ominously.

'This is no time for tea!' said Georgie gaily. 'Nick put some champagne in the fridge to chill as soon as we knew everything was all right. Go and get it, darling,' she added to her husband. 'We've got so much to celebrate!'

As Nick disappeared obediently, Georgie tucked a hand through Chase's arm and kissed him on the cheek where a muscle still jumped furiously. 'I have to say we were both a bit hurt you didn't let us know,' she said reproachfully.

'You must have known that we'd want to be there for your wedding.'

'I didn't tell you because it wasn't important,' said Chase, biting the words out in an effort to restrain his temper.

Charming! thought Bea bitterly.

Startled, Georgie took her arm out of his and stared at him. 'What?'

'Chloe doesn't understand the situation, I'm afraid,' he said curtly. 'Our marriage was a purely practical arrangement so that Bea could stay in Australia. Your busybody cousin could have saved herself a phone call and you and Nick could have had that holiday in Mexico!'

Georgie looked from him to Bea with a puzzled expression. 'Is this true?'

'Absolutely.' Bea bared her teeth in a smile. Since Chase was being brutally honest, there was no need for her to pretend, either, was there? 'Marriage was just a way for me to get round visa restrictions, and we agreed to get a divorce as soon as you came home. In fact, we were discussing that just now, weren't we, Chase?'

'We were,' he agreed with something of a snap. 'Neither of us can wait!'

'Here we go!' Nick reappeared, flourishing champagne and glasses, but he stopped as he picked up the tense atmosphere and looked from Chase to Bea to his wife. 'Have I missed something?'

'Bea and I were just explaining to Georgie that we only married on the understanding that it wouldn't be permanent,' Chase told him tightly. 'Bea's only stayed here to look after Chloe until you came home, and now that you *are* home, she's going to be heading for Sydney as soon as possible.'

'Are you really going to Sydney?' Georgie asked Bea later when she joined her in the kitchen after putting Chloe to bed.

'That was the deal.' Bea had herself well under control now. 'I want to set up a catering business.' If she said it often enough, she might even remember why.

Georgie sat down at the table. 'What about you and Chase?'

'It was only ever a temporary thing,' said Bea, managing a careless shrug. 'I'm very grateful to Chase. If he hadn't married me, I would be back in London by now.'

'So it really was just a practical arrangement?'

Bea thought about the nights she and Chase had spent learning each other's bodies, the joy and the laughter and the rocketing excitement. 'Yes.'

'You wouldn't think about staying a bit longer?' Georgie suggested delicately.

'There's no point,' said Bea, lifting the casserole out of the oven and making a show of tasting it. 'It's not as if either of us have planned a future together.'

'Why not?'

'I'm sure Erin told you how unsuitable I am!'

'Oh, Erin!' Georgie rolled her eyes. 'What does she know? She's spent a lot of time over the years telling me how unsuitable I am too. I mean, look at me!'

She gestured disparagingly down at herself. There were pearls at her throat and glittering rings on her fingers, and she was wearing a shirt and a pair of trousers, both made of some pale, silky material and beautifully cut. They had absolutely nothing in common with the shirts and trousers Erin had worn.

'Do I look suitable to you?' she asked Bea.

Bea went back to her casserole. 'Erin says you can ride.'

'Yes, I can ride, but Nick doesn't need a wife who can ride. I don't help out with branding and castrating and those other horrible things they do in the yards. I don't do any of the things

Erin thinks makes you a suitable wife, but that doesn't matter to Nick.'

'It matters to Chase,' said Bea before she could help herself.

'He might think so, but he's wrong. All he needs is a wife who loves him. It's too easy to forget that,' Georgie went on soberly. 'That's what Nick and I did, and it nearly cost us our marriage. When I left Calulla Downs last time, I didn't think I would ever come back. I thought I couldn't be the kind of wife Nick wanted, or the kind of mother Chloe needed, and that they'd both be better off without me, but I was wrong.'

A reminiscent smile curved her lovely lips as if remembering how Nick had put her right on just what he wanted. 'It turns out they both like me the way I am!'

'Does that mean you'll be giving up your career?' asked Bea.

'No,' Georgie shook her head. 'Acting is important to me, and I need to be able to do it, but from now on, I'm only going to do one film a year, and Nick and Chloe will come with me. The rest of the time we'll be here, doing what Nick needs to do.'

'I'm glad you've been able to work something out,' said Bea honestly.

'You and Chase could work something out, too.'

She shook her head. 'It's different for us.'

'Is it?' asked Georgie. 'You both just need to decide what you really want, not what Erin thinks you ought to want.'

'We know what we want.' Bea took a deep breath. 'I want to go back to Sydney, and Chase wants Wilbara.'

If she said it often enough and firmly enough, maybe Georgie would accept it.

Maybe *she* would accept it.

'I can't see myself spending my life in the outback,' she made herself say lightly, casually, as if she were talking about a pair of shoes and not about a whole future without Chase. 'Certainly not at a place like Wilbara.'

'Of course you can't live at Wilbara,' Nick said, coming into the kitchen with Chase in time to hear the end of their conversation. 'The place is a ruin. I've been trying to talk Chase out of it,' he told Georgie. 'I've suggested we split Calulla Downs and build him a house of his own.'

Georgie's face lit up. 'Oh, that's a wonderful idea!' she cried, and Nick's hand rested in a brief, revealing caress on his wife's hair.

'I know, but Chase won't hear of it,' he grumbled. 'He's insisting on Wilbara. Can't you talk him out of it, Bea?' he appealed to her, evidently placing as little belief as Georgie in their protestations that theirs was simply a marriage of convenience. 'Make him see sense!'

'It's nothing to do with Bea,' said Chase flatly before she could answer. 'She's going to Sydney.'

'Let me have your address when you get to Sydney, and I'll contact you about the divorce,' said Chase.

The Sydney plane was half an hour late, and they were sitting side by side on the plastic chairs at Mackinnon airport. Bea's hair was styled straight and smooth again, and she was wearing a short skirt, cropped top and her favourite shoes. If she had to go back to the city, she was going back in style, she had decided.

It was just as well it was ending like this, before she had time to do anything really silly like deciding that she was in love with Chase after all. It had been touch and go there for a while, but fortunately yesterday had shown her just how unpleasant and unreasonable and downright difficult he could be!

Bea had spent the night back in the room she had once shared with Emily, telling herself it was all for the best. Chase was in a foul mood because she hadn't raved about Wilbara, but why had he asked her to go with him if he hadn't wanted her opinion? It wasn't even as if he had suggested she might have some stake in the place. He hadn't even *considered* asking her to stay on until the Wet.

No one in their right minds would want to spend the rest of their life stuck in the middle of nowhere, with only Wal, assorted creepy-crawlies, and a man like that.

'I'll write to you as soon as soon as I find somewhere to live,' she told Chase in a brittle voice. 'Shall I send it to Calulla Downs, or are you planning to move to Wilbara straight away?'

'Send it to Wilbara,' said Chase. 'I'll be there.'

'Right.'

Bea tugged off her wedding ring and gave it back to him. 'Here,' she said, flinching inwardly as if she had torn off a piece of her flesh, 'I nearly forgot.'

The skin around Chase's mouth seemed to tighten, but he barely glanced at the ring as he put it in the pocket of his shirt. 'It might be sensible to leave it a little while in case the immigration authorities get suspicious,' he said, his voice empty of all expression, 'but if you meet someone else and want to speed things up, let me know.'

Bea tried to imagine herself meeting another man. She hadn't had much luck so far, what with Phil and now Chase. Maybe it would be third time lucky, she thought gloomily, but it was impossible to picture right now.

Still, Chase might have his own reasons for wanting to be officially single again. 'You too,' she said.

There was another long, bitter silence. Bea stared desperately at the sky, willing the plane to appear, but as soon as it did, she was gripped by panic at the realisation that she was going to have to say goodbye to him.

Suddenly, everything was happening quickly. Too quickly. The plane had landed and there was a bustle of activity on the tarmac as steps were pushed out, passengers disembarked and the trailer loaded with her solitary suitcase trundled out to the cargo hold.

Now the official was opening the door. 'The plane's just about ready to go,' he called cheerfully, and the two other passengers who had been waiting headed over and joked with him as he tore the stubs off their boarding cards.

Somehow, Bea got to her feet. Chase was standing too, his face closed and bleak. He picked up her bag and gave it to her.

He was going to let her go, Bea realised incredulously. Until now, she hadn't really believed that it would happen. This, then, was it.

She took a shaky breath. 'Well…good luck with Wilbara,' she managed.

'Good luck with your business.' A muscle was beating in Chase's jaw, but otherwise his face might have been carved from stone. 'Thank you for all your hard work,' he added stiffly.

'I should be thanking you for marrying me,' said Bea. 'I wouldn't be able to stay in Australia if it hadn't been for you.'

'I'm glad you got what you wanted,' said Chase bleakly.

Bea didn't even have the heart to pretend that it was true. She hoisted her bag onto her shoulder. 'I…I'd better go,' she said and stepped back before she could throw herself into his arms and beg him to let her stay.

Terrified that she was going to cry, she put on her sunglasses with fumbling fingers and headed blindly towards the door, where the official tore off her boarding card and handed her back the stub.

'Have a good flight,' he beamed.

Bea nodded dumbly, took a step towards the door, and then hesitated. Involuntarily, she looked back at Chase. He was standing there, watching her go, with an expression so stony that her heart cracked.

'Goodbye, Bea,' he said.

Bea tried to smile in return, but it didn't work, and she turned quickly to step through the door before he could see her mouth shaking. The tears trickled down her cheeks from beneath her sunglasses as she walked across the hot tarmac, and this time she didn't look back.

'I'm worried about you,' Emily declared.

She had turned up in Sydney three weeks after Bea, having discovered that her laid-back diving instructor was so laid-back that he had forgotten to mention that he already had a girlfriend back home in Brisbane.

'Another Prince Charming who turns out to be a frog in disguise,' she said cheerfully to Bea, who envied her ability to fall disastrously in love so many times without losing her belief that the right man was waiting for her just around the corner. She was already making eyes at the manager of the bar where she had picked up a job.

'You seem a bit down,' Emily went on. 'I thought you'd be thrilled about being back in Sydney and able to stay in Australia.' She looked at Bea with a puzzled expression. 'You're not missing Chase, are you?'

It was like a dentist drilling on a nerve. Bea flinched inwardly. The truth was that she *was* missing Chase. She was missing him more than she would have believed possible.

She had arrived back in Sydney in high dudgeon, infuriated by his attitude and determined to put the whole episode behind her. Whatever she had felt for him had been mere physical attraction, Bea decided, and even that had vanished when she realised just how stubborn and pigheaded he could be. As soon as she got back to the city she would forget all about him, right?

Wrong.

Bea couldn't forget. She couldn't forget the way he stamped the dust from his boots, the way he hung up his hat, the way he smiled when he pulled her into his arms.

She couldn't forget those quiet evenings on the veranda and the sound of his voice in the darkness. She couldn't forget the sleek strength of his body and how his chest vibrated when he held her to him and laughed. Bea's heart clenched with longing whenever she thought about it.

Six weeks she had been back in Sydney now. Six weeks of missing Chase, six weeks of needing him, aching for his touch, aching just to be near him.

Six weeks of realising that she loved him.

She had wanted it to be a physical thing but it was more than that, Bea knew that now. It didn't matter how different they were. Chase was part of her, and without him she felt incomplete. She just didn't know what to do about it.

'You don't belong,' Chase had said. 'I'm holding out for a suitable girl.'

He would never think that she was suitable, not after that day at Wilbara. She had been childish, hysterical, and frivolous, not an appealing combination at the best of times, let alone when she had been busy pouring cold water over his plans and recoiling from a bit of dirt and neglect. No wonder Chase had been glad to see her go.

She could have encouraged him, Bea thought now that it was too late. She could have told him how exciting it would be to rebuild

Wilbara and make it a home again. She could have told him straight out that she wanted to do it with him.

But she hadn't. She had screamed and sneered and run away from a spider instead.

That spider had been horrible, Bea tried to be fair to herself. She wasn't sure that she would ever get used to all those creepy-crawlies. It would take courage to live in a place like Wilbara.

But not as much courage as she would need to get through life without Chase.

Bea had made up her mind. She had booked a seat on a plane back to Mackinnon that week-end. She was going to find Chase and tell him that she loved him and beg him to give her another chance. He might say no, but at least she would have tried.

She hadn't told Emily yet. She didn't want her exclaiming and teasing or crowing that she had known all along. She just wanted Chase. She wanted him so badly that sometimes she felt sick and giddy with the longing just to see him again.

One more night of work, and she would be on her way. Without the heart to set up business on her own, Bea had contacted her old company who had welcomed her back with open arms, and she had passed on the contacts Georgie had given her before she left.

'Strictly A-list parties only, darling,' Georgie had promised. 'I'll recommend you.'

One of Georgie's friends was having a party that night in Elizabeth Bay, and Bea was going to supervise the finishing touches to the food.

Wearing a plain black, sleeveless dress, she moved through the throng with her exquisite delicacies, smiling mechanically as she offered the tray to people who hardly noticed that she was there. The chatter was deafening, and longing for the silence of the outback stabbed at her like a knife twisting in her side.

One more day, she reminded herself.

Through the crowds she glimpsed a solitary figure on the edge of the room, looking out into the garden as if hating the party as much as she was. Bea headed that way, desperate suddenly to get out of the crush of bodies and clashing perfumes.

'Would you like—?'

She broke off in stunned disbelief as the man swung round at the sound of her voice. The tray started to slide and would have fallen from her nerveless hands if he hadn't caught it and straightened it for her.

'*Chase*?' Bea stared at him hungrily, unable to believe that it was really him. He was thinner and tauter and out of place in this glittering, glamorous setting, but it was him, it *was*! 'Wh-what are you doing here?' she stammered.

'The hostess is a friend of Georgie's,' he said, his voice sounding strange in his own ears. 'I told her that I was going to be in Sydney and she asked if I wanted to come, so I did.'

'I thought you hated this kind of thing!'

Chase didn't answer. He couldn't take his eyes off Bea. In that little black dress, with her hair smoothed behind her ears she looked alarmingly sophisticated, but there was an air of fragility about her, as if she were tensed against a blow, and he could see shadows beneath her beautiful eyes.

He didn't know how to begin. Four of these horrible parties he had endured before this one, passed around from one of Georgie's friends to another in the hope that someone would have been in contact with Bea. He had dreamt of finding her again, and now here she was, and all the careful speeches he had rehearsed had deserted him.

'You said you would let me know where you were.'

It came out more accusingly than he had intended, and Bea's eyes slid away from his.

'I'm sorry,' she muttered. Now was not the time to tell him that she hadn't wanted him to contact her about a divorce. 'I...I meant to be in touch, but I've been busy.'

'I've been trying to find you,' said Chase. 'I need to talk to you.'

He sounded so serious that Bea's entrails tangled themselves into a tight knot of fear. *Get in contact if you meet someone else*, he had said. *You too*, she had replied, never believing that he would.

Oh, God, was that why he was here? *Had* he found someone else? Had she left it too late?

'What about?' she asked through stiff lips.

Chase opened his mouth to reply when a burst of laughter from a group nearby distracted them both. A girl who had clearly had rather too much to drink was shrieking and giggling as the young men around her attempted to lob canapés down her cleavage.

'We can't talk here,' said Chase, raking his fingers through his hair in frustration. 'Let's get out of here.'

Bea was still clutching her tray. 'I'm supposed to be working,' she said doubtfully.

'You think anyone here is going to notice if you're not here for a few minutes?' said Chase with something of his old style.

He was right. The party was in full swing and there were other waitresses circulating, although nobody seemed to be eating any more. No one would miss her.

Bea followed Chase out through the sliding doors onto a terrace. The garden was beautifully landscaped down a hillside, and a swimming pool gleamed in the moonlight below. Nothing but the best for Georgie's friends.

Setting down her tray on a table, she walked with him down the steps to a curving poolside terrace where they could sit in the shadows under a vine-draped pergola. For several minutes they sat there, not talking, not speaking. In fact, Chase was silent for so long that Bea wondered whether he'd forgotten that he wanted to talk to her.

The silence, at first comforting, began to jangle. Bea hugged her arms together and sought for something to say.

'How's Chloe?' she managed eventually.

'Fine.'

'And Georgie and Nick?'

'They're fine too.'

Another pause.

'How's Georgie getting on with the cooking?' Bea asked.

'We've got a new cook.'

'Oh.' Bea bit her lip, unprepared for the twist of pain at the knowledge that they had replaced her so easily. 'What's she like?'

'She's very good,' said Chase. He seemed relieved that the conversation had got going at last. 'Her name's Morag. She's Scottish, and grew up on a farm, so she feels quite at home in the outback.'

Bea didn't want to know that. She wanted to know whether Morag was pretty.

'Is she nice?' she asked jealously.

'Very nice.'

How nice? Bea wanted to shout. Nice enough for him to want to spend the rest of his life with her? Was Morag the one?

Her heart churned as she sat next to Chase on the bench. After that burst of information about Morag, he seemed to have run out of inspiration, and he was clearly struggling to find the right words to say what he had come for.

This was it, Bea braced herself, but as he opened his mouth, she stumbled into speech before he could say what he wanted.

'How…how are things at Wilbara?' she asked breathlessly. Anything to put off the moment of truth for as long as she could.

He turned slowly to look at her. 'I didn't buy Wilbara,' he told her.

'Didn't buy it?' Bea repeated blankly. 'Why not?'

'I was thinking I might like to spend some time in Sydney,' said Chase. As if aware of how awkward he sounded, he stopped and cleared his throat. 'Maybe get a job down here for a while.'

She stared at him, unable to believe that she had heard him properly. 'You want to come to Sydney?' she said very carefully, and then, when Chase just nodded, '*Why*?'

He glanced away, disconcerted by the incredulity in her face. It didn't make it any easier when you knew that this was the last thing she had been expecting or wanting to hear.

'I thought that if I was here, I might be able to see you sometimes,' he said with some difficulty, wishing that he could remember some of those fine speeches he had prepared to tell her how he felt. 'I thought…I thought it might be easier just being near you.'

'Near *me*?' Bea whispered, terrified that if she moved or spoke too loudly this would turn out to be no more than a dream.

'Yes.'

'I thought you'd come about the divorce,' she said.

'No.' Chase shook his head. 'That is, I did in a way. I wanted to ask you if we could forget the divorce,' he told her. 'I wondered if we could begin again like normal people. I know how much you want to stay in Sydney, Bea, so I thought if I got a job, even if you don't want to live together, we could see each other, couldn't we?'

He was stumbling over his words by then, desperate to persuade her, to hear her say yes. 'If it doesn't work, we could still divorce,' he said. 'If that's what you want.'

Bea just sat there and stared at him, her heart too full to speak, shaking her head at the sheer wonder of it.

Chase misinterpreted her silence. 'I just want you to give me another chance, Bea,' he said urgently. 'I know I don't deserve it. Georgie told me how unpleasant I was that day you left, but you've got to understand how angry I was. Angry with you for hating Wilbara, and angry with me for pretending you would ever think about living there.'

When Bea still said nothing, he leant forward to rest his arms on his knees, not looking at her.

'I was stupid and selfish and too stubborn to admit how much I needed you,' he confessed. 'I tried telling myself that I would get over you, but it didn't work.'

He smiled crookedly, remembering his attempts to forget her. 'When I went back to Wilbara, it was desolate without you and Wal kept asking where you were, and when you'd be coming back, and what I thought you'd want doing to the homestead until I couldn't stand it any longer. I told him we'd decided not to buy the property, and went home to tell Nick and Georgie I was coming to find you.

'It wasn't that easy, though,' he went on, thinking about the last few desperate days. 'You hadn't let me know your address, so the only thing I could think of was to try all Georgie's friends to see if any of them had heard from you. Nobody knew your name, but everyone said to come along when they were using caterers and maybe one of the waitresses would know you.

'This is the fifth of these parties I've been to in three days,' said Chase. 'I was nearly ready to give up and try another way when I turned round just now, and suddenly there you were.'

He had been watching the pool, but at that he glanced up into Bea's face. 'There you were,' he repeated simply.

Bea swallowed. 'You said you didn't love me,' she said slowly.

'I lied,' said Chase, his eyes going back to the water. 'I didn't want you to feel pressurised. I told myself that it wouldn't last, and that when you went I would somehow stop loving you, but I didn't.'

He straightened, and looked directly into her eyes. 'I missed you,' he said.

Warmth was spilling along Bea's veins like sunshine, melting the cold knot of misery inside her.

'I said I didn't love you either,' she reminded him quietly.

'I know. I'm not asking you for anything you can't give,' Chase promised her. 'I just want to be with you.'

A smile trembled on Bea's lips as she reached out and laid a gentle hand on his shoulder. 'The thing is, Chase, I lied too,' she said. 'I didn't tell you the truth.'

'The truth?'

'The truth, that I'm in love with you.'

'Bea...' Chase searched her face with eyes that were suddenly alight with hope. '*Bea*,' he said again, and his arm came round her to pull her onto his lap. 'Bea, say that again.'

Her arms wound round his neck. 'I love you.'

And then at last they could kiss, deep, desperate kisses to banish the memory of the long weeks when they had needed each other and the future had seemed dark and empty.

'I love you...I love you...I love you,' Bea gasped between kisses, pressing her lips to his ear, to his jaw, to his mouth again, boneless and giddy with joy and relief and the dazzling delight of knowing that he loved her too.

'Why didn't you tell me this before?' Chase pretended to grumble, his arms tight around her. 'We've wasted all this time!'

'Why didn't you tell me?' she countered.

'I wasn't sure that you were really over Phil,' he said slowly. 'He hurt you a lot.'

Bea lifted her head at that, and sat back slightly so that she could look into his face. 'Yes, he did,' she agreed, 'but if he hadn't, I would never have found you and realised what love really was. When it happened, I thought my world had ended, but now I know that it hadn't ended at all, it was just beginning. Now I know that you can't be truly happy unless you're with the right person. The right person for Phil is Anna,' she said, accepting at last that this was true, 'and the right person for me is you.'

And she kissed Chase, a warm, sweet kiss to seal her promise.

Some time later, when she was resting her face against his throat and breathing in the familiar scent of his skin, she fingered the buttons on his shirt. 'What about you?' she asked a little anxiously. 'You're over Georgie, aren't you?'

Chase pulled back his head to stare at her blankly. 'Georgie?'

'I was afraid that you might still be a tiny bit in love with her,' Bea confessed. 'Erin kept saying how much you adored her.'

'I've been over Georgie a long time, Bea,' he told her. 'At the time, I thought I loved her, it's true, but it was never quite real. What I felt for Georgie is nothing like what I feel for you,' he went on, lifting Bea's hand to press a warm kiss into her palm. 'It's not something I can put into words, it's just knowing that we belong together, and that without you, nothing would ever feel quite…right. You know that, too, don't you?'

Deeply satisfied, Bea nodded, but couldn't resist teasing as she wound her arms around his neck. 'Even though you really wanted a suitable girl?'

'There's only one suitable girl for me,' said Chase, kissing her again, 'and she's right here where she belongs!'

Bea rested her head back on his shoulder with a blissful sigh and he smoothed the hair from her face tenderly.

'So, wife, can we go back to being married again?'

'We can,' she said happily.

'Let's go and look for a house tomorrow,' he said. 'Wherever you like.'

Bea sat up out of the circle of his arms. 'There's a bit of a problem,' she told him, her face serious.

'What?'

'I don't think you'd like living in Sydney.'

'I would if you were here with me,' Chase insisted.

'That's just it,' said Bea. 'I won't be here. I'm leaving Sydney the day after tomorrow. I've booked my flight and everything.'

Chase stilled in dismay. 'Where are you going?' A terrible thought struck him. 'Not back to England?'

'Well, there's nothing definite yet,' she told him, 'but I *did* hear that there was a property near Mackinnon which badly needs a housekeeper. The homestead needs a lot of work, I gather, but I like the idea of making it into a home, and I was sort of hoping that if I was very nice to the owner, he might make the position permanent. Of course, that was before I heard that he was stupidly thinking of throwing it all in and moving to Sydney of all places!'

It was Chase's turn to stare in disbelief.

'You want to come to Wilbara?' he asked carefully, just to check that he understood.

Bea smiled at him lovingly. 'It's where you're going to be, isn't it?'

'But…you're a city girl. You hate the outback.'

'That's what I said,' she admitted, 'but that wasn't true either. Oh, I have to admit that I'm not that keen on the flies and I really don't like the spiders at all, but I don't hate them nearly as much as I love you.'

A smile started in Chase's eyes and spread over his whole face. 'You love me that much?'

'More than that,' said Bea, and melted back against him for a long, sweet kiss. 'Much more than that,' she mumbled against his lips. 'Much, much more.'

'Bea, are you sure?' said Chase some time later. 'Wilbara's no place for you. It's dirty and uncomfortable and falling to pieces.'

'Then we'll just have to clean it and put it together again.'

'It will be hard work,' he warned.

'I know, but we'll do it together,' she said as she kissed him. 'It will be worth it.'

Chase still wasn't convinced. 'What about all the creepy-crawlies?'

'Wal can deal with them.'

'Seriously, Bea,' said Chase, longing to believe her but determined to make sure she understood just what she was letting herself in for while she still had a chance to change her mind. 'Wilbara hasn't even got basic essentials at the moment, and it's miles from everything a girl like you needs.'

'You mean like shops and bars and cinemas?'

'Yes, that kind of thing.' Seized by fresh doubt, Chase gloomily contemplated how little he could offer Bea. It would be better to live in Sydney than watch her pining for the city.

But Bea was putting her arms around his neck and her lips were warm below his ear. 'I've learnt that a lot of things I used to think were essential aren't that important,' she told him.

It felt so good, so right, to be holding her again that Chase let his last lingering doubts dissolve in the intoxicating promise of the future they would share.

'You'd be surprised at how little I need now,' she murmured, her kisses drifting enticingly along his jaw.

Chase started to smile as his arms tightened around her. 'Just somewhere to plug in your hair-dryer?' he suggested wickedly, and Bea laughed as she kissed him once more.

'And you,' she said.

MILLS & BOON® PUBLISH EIGHT LARGE PRINT TITLES A MONTH. THESE ARE THE EIGHT TITLES FOR MARCH 2003

❦
————————————————

HOT PURSUIT
Anne Mather

WIFE: BOUGHT AND PAID FOR
Jacqueline Baird

THE FORCED MARRIAGE
Sara Craven

MACKENZIE'S PROMISE
Catherine Spencer

MAYBE MARRIED
Leigh Michaels

THE TYCOON'S PROPOSITION
Rebecca Winters

THE WEDDING CHALLENGE
Jessica Hart

ASSIGNMENT: SINGLE MAN
Caroline Anderson

MILLS & BOON®

0203 Rom

MILLS & BOON® PUBLISH EIGHT LARGE PRINT TITLES A MONTH. THESE ARE THE EIGHT TITLES FOR APRIL 2003

❦

THE GREEK BRIDEGROOM
Helen Bianchin

THE ARABIAN LOVE-CHILD
Michelle Reid

CHRISTMAS AT HIS COMMAND
Helen Brooks

FINN'S PREGNANT BRIDE
Sharon Kendrick

OUTBACK ANGEL
Margaret Way

HIS PRETEND WIFE
Lucy Gordon

CITY GIRL IN TRAINING
Liz Fielding

BRIDEGROOM ON HER DOORSTEP
Renee Roszel

MILLS & BOON®

0303 Rom LP